VENTURER—TOP SECRET

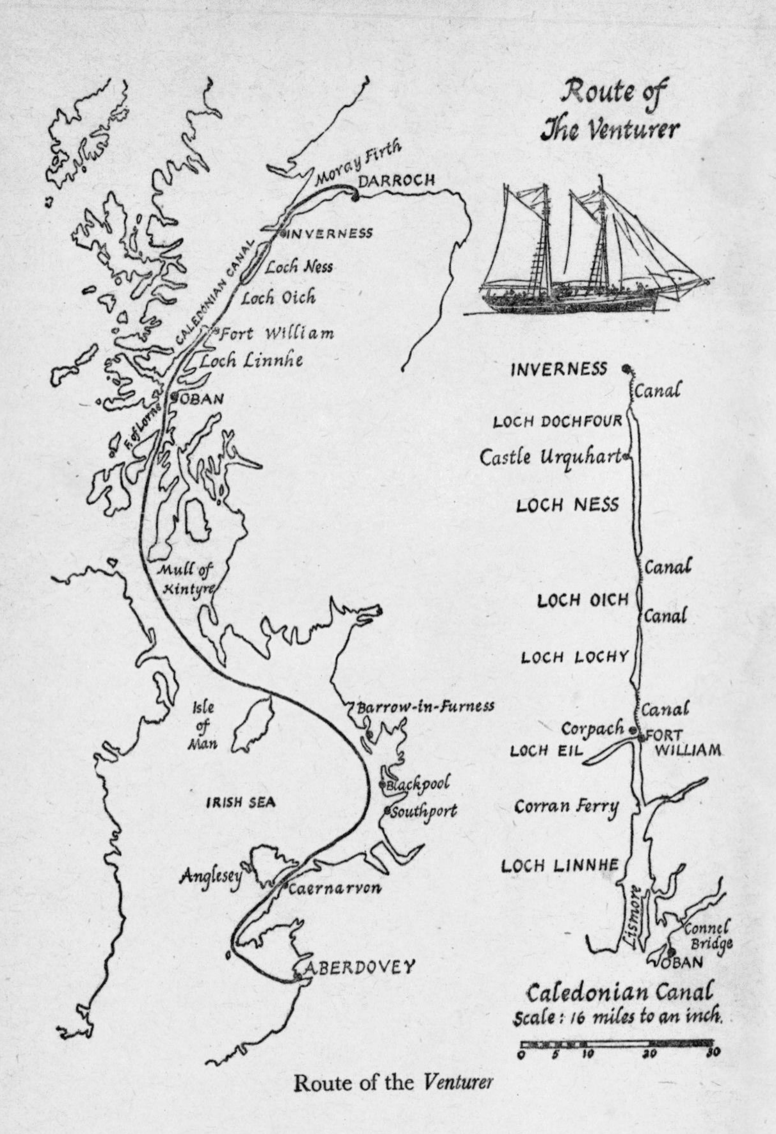

Route of the *Venturer*

VENTURER
TOP SECRET

by

IAN SIME

Illustrated by Robert Hodgson

THOMAS NELSON AND SONS LTD
LONDON EDINBURGH PARIS MELBOURNE JOHANNESBURG
TORONTO AND NEW YORK

THOMAS NELSON AND SONS LTD

Parkside Works Edinburgh 9
36 Park Street London W1
312 Flinders Street Melbourne C1

302–304 Barclays Bank Building
Commissioner and Kruis Streets
Johannesburg

Thomas Nelson and Sons (Canada) Ltd
91–93 Wellington Street West Toronto 1

Thomas Nelson and Sons
19 East 47th Street New York 17

Société Française d'Éditions Nelson
97 rue Monge Paris 5

CONTENTS

LIST OF ILLUSTRATIONS

CHAPTER I

A NIGHT TO REMEMBER

'LOOK out, someone is coming up the stairs!'

For an instant all was pandemonium in the Big Dorm of St Mark's as Jackie Main's urgent whisper took effect. Cakes vanished, saucers of fruit seemed to melt into thin air while biscuits and tins of condensed milk found temporary cover beneath the sheets. Squeak Naylor, unable to clear the maze of wires which surrounded his crystal set, had to go to earth with the head-phones round his neck and the bedclothes pulled up till they almost suffocated him.

In a remarkably short time all was as it should have been on that summer evening in 1941. Term was half over, and after nearly a year the School was well settled into its new surroundings in mid-Wales. The evacuation from their homes on the shore of the Moray Firth had certainly disorganised the routine, but it had also stimulated the boys. If the staff were worried, the boys, at least the Mids and Juniors, thought the whole thing tremendous fun.

Over in the far corner a bed rattled as a heavy body eased itself to a new position.

'Shut up, you fool. You'll get us all caught. You really are an idiot. Have you no sense at all?' Timothy Ballard, the Vice-Room-leader, hissed at the culprit.

'I can't help it,' wailed Percy. 'The chocolate icing is soaking through my pyjamas.'

'Might have known it,' snorted Timothy. 'You can always rely on Percy Chester to muck things up somehow. You goat!'

Timothy emphasised his point by hurling a slipper at the luckless Percy. The aim was good, just what you would expect from the first XI reserve. Just how good was seen when Percy leapt from his bed with a loud cry to scrape a mixture of cake and chocolate icing from his bare tummy.

'It's not funny,' he growled, as the rest of his room mates rocked with suppressed laughter.

'No?' giggled Jackie. 'You can't see yourself.'

'That's enough from you. For a first-term kid you have a darned sight too much to say for yourself. If you had been any good at your job of Guard we wouldn't have had a blooming false alarm and I——'

'Oh, pipe down, Percy, and get on with it! We all know that as a first termer you distinguished yourself by getting your dorm caught three nights running—once with a whole chicken in the middle of the floor.'

Chester went crimson and immediately lapsed into silence. Ballard had been in the School too long for his comfort. He knew too much and had an unhappy knack of recalling each *faux pas* of Percy's in great detail.

However, Percy could not keep silent for long.

'You'll never guess what I heard,' he said.

'Was it interesting?' Timothy speared another chunk of pineapple from the fruit salad tin with the point of a compass.

'Of course it was. I heard it when I was

operating the telephone switchboard during lunch —you stinker! ' Percy broke off short to aim a blow at young Groundwater who had shipped a plum from under his nose while he had been speaking. But he didn't care about the loss of the plum. What did matter was that he had side-tracked the conversation away from the chicken fiasco—if only Ballard didn't set them on him again. He gave the Vice-Room-leader a quick look to see how the wind stood, but that worthy was much too busy trying to spear an evasive cherry to enter deeply into the conversation.

Percy pressed his advantage. ' It was like this,' he went on : ' I had just taken over from Betty, who had gone off leaving her usual host of idiotic instructions, when a call came in for the Head on one of the outside lines.'

' Chester, you didn't listen in, did you? You know each operator is trusted. I never would have thought it of you. Why——'

' Close down, Squeak.' Percy rounded on the radio enthusiast. ' You're so goody-goody, that one day it will kill you. And I didn't listen in, if you want to know—not intentionally at any rate.'

' Ah, I know your type,' Squeak scoffed. ' Accidentally on purpose like.'

' Look, if you don't clew up, I'll come over and tickle you with your own cat's whisker. What's more, with the earth in one ear and the aerial shoved down the other, that apology of a brain of yours will be short-circuited.' Percy was by this time out of bed and advancing on Naylor, determined to re-establish his prestige.

But Squeak was no fighter. He loved his set too

much and would take anything so long as it remained intact. ' All right, I'm sorry. I was only pulling your leg. You don't have to get so steamed up,' he said.

' Promise ? ' Percy glowered from the end of the bed.

' Promise,' Naylor replied, glad that nothing worse had come of it.

But he had misjudged his opponent. With speed quite surprising for one of his size and shape—he was the heaviest in Lower School—Percy dodged round the end of the bed and playfully tousled Squeak's blond hair with his huge hand.

' All right then, my little Marconi, we'll say it's quits, for the time being. You call up the fairies on that juke box of yours and tell them Uncle Percy has let you off.'

He released his hold, bounded off back to bed and had all but reached it before the whole room heaved with subdued mirth. He turned to enjoy the effect of his efforts. There sat Squeak in his usual tangle of wires, head-phones askew, with the remains of a very over-ripe plum slowly trickling down over his face from his ruffled hair.

' Never mind, they say it grows hair on eggs, if rubbed well in,' Jackie chortled.

Squeak, almost speechless with rage, was about to reply when the she-bear's voice echoed down the corridors. Miss Derwent, the House Matron, was a lady of no small stature, who struck terror into the hearts of even prefects.

He was still fuming gently when Chester and Ballard unceremoniously shoved his head under the clothes, bundled his apparatus on top and smoothed out the covers.

They just made their beds again, sliding quietly down the very outside edge of the mattresses so that the creaking of the springs wouldn't give them away, when Miss Derwent reached the linen locker in the passage outside.

For what seemed to be a terribly long time she examined towels and rearranged the linen. Beneath the sheets Squeak was rapidly running out of air, but each time that he tried to raise the covers just a little the box of the set clanged against the ebonite of his head-phones and earned him a terrific dig from the fellow in the next bed.

Moreover, the plum was more than half bad, so that the stench from it, together with the smell of the rubber-covered wires and his bay-rum hair lotion combined to produce an atmosphere strongly suggestive of the sixth form chemie lab. To add to his discomfort he was getting cramp in his left leg. Just when he was certain that he could stand no more, the bedclothes were pulled back and Ballard stood grinning down at him.

'Come on, it's safe now. The she-bear has gone off to her lair. Cor, what a mess you're in. You had better nip off to the bathroom and see what you can do about it.'

To the accompaniment of many and varied ribald remarks, Squeak got clear of his set and made his way out.

'Percy, what did happen in the telephone exchange?' Groundwater asked.

'As I said. Betty, the operator, had gone to lunch leaving——'

'Yes, we got all that before,' Timothy cut in. 'Do come to the point.'

Chester gave him a scornful look. 'If Dr Ballard does not wish to harken to my words of wisdom . . .'

Timothy let fly with his other slipper, scoring another direct hit on the fleshiest part of Percy's posterior.

'You great mound of vibrating blubber,' he said as he regained his squatting position. 'It's little wonder you float like a seal in the swimming pond. I'll "Dr Ballard" you in a minute. Get on with this rumour of yours.'

'It wasn't a rumour,' replied Chester, rubbing his target area. 'It was a telegram from someone in the Admiralty.'

'In the Admiralty?' echoed Jackie in a slightly awed voice.

'Yes, the Admiralty.' Percy nodded his head slowly with each word, savouring the importance of his news. 'I took it down and sent it up to the Head.'

'You did?' Timothy looked highly sceptical. 'Knowing your flare for getting everything the wrong way round, you have probably despatched the fleet to the Tagus by now. You will be popular.'

'Don't be a bigger ass than nature intended you should be. The message was quite simple. It said: "Permission granted. Confirmatory letter following".'

'Honest?' asked Timothy.

'Honest.'

'Wonder what on earth that can have been. Must have something to do with the seamanship.'

Timothy was keen on sailing and had just started to be of some use in a boat, when war was declared and the Moray Firth was closed to all small craft.

'Hey, Percy,' he called. 'What did the Head say when he got the message?'

'Don't know. I didn't deliver it. Young Wallace took it up.'

'You have no idea what it's all about? Seriously now, no fooling,' he added as Percy got ready for some smart reply.

'Hey, wait a moment,' chipped in Jackie. 'My brother wrote me the other day to say that some strangers, city types he called them, had been looking over the *Venturer* in Darroch harbour. He heard one say that someone would have to dig away a mighty lot of sand before she could be moved. He thought she might be up for sale now that the School had been moved so far away.'

'Old Dreaver would never let them sell the *Venturer*. She is his pride and joy. Remember all the fuss after she had been bought from the Sea Scouts at Scarborough. She had to be renamed with all due pomp and ceremony,' said Timothy. 'That was just after I came. I can't remember who broke the bottle, but she was an elderly lady, quite regal to look at and the whole thing had some deep significance because the *Venturer* had once been a pilot boat on the river Weiser.

'Her sails are stamped W.P.—Weiser Pilot—to this day. But you are off the beam, Jackie. This wire can't have anything to do with the *Venturer*. She's there till the war is over, I reckon. No good for transport or anything and anyway she's quite old.'

'Aye, that she may be,' Jackie agreed, 'but she is all sheathed in copper below the water line, you know. I've seen her at low water when she is high and dry.'

'Do you mean to say you can walk right up under her stern?' asked Groundwater.

'You bet you can, and you can turn the propellers if you try hard enough.' Jackie knew—hadn't he done it and got a belting from his Dad for his troubles?—but he left that part out.

Again footsteps were heard approaching up the corridor, but most of the mess had already been cleared and it only remained for everyone to slip quietly down in bed to create an illusion of peace. There was a clatter of something falling and the steps stopped as the owner obviously tried to pick it up.

'Bah! I might have guessed it.' Percy bounced up in bed again. 'Poor old Squeak and his massive ear-phones. Here, you fellows, watch this.' He jumped up on a chair behind the door armed with a pillow which he held, poised above his head.

As Naylor came in, his hair still soaking wet from his attempts to get rid of the plum, Ballard attracted his attention by asking him how he got on. He stopped just inside the door long enough for Percy to strike. But school pillows being what they were, and Chester having no mean force at his command, the worst happened. The pillow split from end to end and in an instant the room was full of feathers. When the cloud settled, there stood Squeak in the middle, with the 'phones round his neck and his hair all covered in down.

'Mummy's ugly duckling, Mummy's ugly duckling!' Jackie started the chant and the rest joined in.

'For goodness' sake, you chaps, cut out the noise,'

Timothy said, drying his own eyes, ' or we will have someone up. And anyway, I think it's time now we packed it in!'

But at the end of twenty minutes, the light had all gone and the worst of the mess had been collected and put in the tin in the housework cupboard. The dorm had settled down and, but for an occasional remark, all was quiet.

Here in the peace of the Welsh countryside, it was hard to imagine that there really was a war on at all. About the only warlike thing they ever saw was the sergeant who came up from the depot of the Welsh Fusiliers to train the Home Guard, and he was a hoot. Only last week he had been trying to take a class in the operation and maintenance of the Browning Light Automatic Rifle. He had learnt the stuff by heart and every time anyone interrupted him he had to go back and start at the beginning again. It had been terrific fun. In a whole afternoon they never got past page one. As soon as he got going, someone asked a question, drawing a good red herring across the trail.

When Blackadder had asked, with an air of utter seriousness, whether, in battle, the equation $S=ut+\frac{1}{2}at^2$ was found to hold good, the poor man finally gave up and sent them all for tea—half an hour early. Unfortunately, on the way over they had run into the Head who had quickly sized things up and had taken steps to occupy the next few Saturday afternoons for the ring-leaders.

It was black dark now and Timothy suddenly found himself wide awake for no very obvious reason at all. Somewhere near at hand two people were talking with lowered voices. He listened carefully and decided that they were those of Tony Gregg and Robin Trenchard, both of whom had been summoned to see the Head after supper.

Gazing intently at the door he thought that he could see part of the shadow darker than the rest but he was unable to make up his mind when the voices stopped, and Gregg came in to get his things from his locker to go down to the bathroom to undress.

As Gregg's footsteps died away down the passage, Timothy heard Percy obviously getting back into bed.

'What are you up to?' he whispered.

'Phew! That was a narrow shave,' Percy replied. 'I had to nip behind the door. Good job he didn't see me. Anyway, it was worth it. I've got all the gen now.' His voice was shaking with excitement.

'Gen? What on?'

'The telegram of course, stupid.'

'Percy, I give up,' said Timothy. 'What are you yattering about?'

'Promise you won't tell anyone,' Percy asked. 'I heard Trenchard say that the Head had told them that it was still secret.'

'If you know it, whatever it is, they might as well have put it on the School board. However, I promise.'

'We were right; the Admiralty have agreed to let the School sail the *Venturer* down from Darroch to Aberdovey by going through the Caledonian Canal. The trip starts at the end of term, and a shipping company is sending a man who is used to sailing ships to be captain. Twelve boys are going as crew and I think he said some other grown-ups but I couldn't be sure.'

Timothy was completely shaken.

'Percy, isn't it wonderful! The Head must have got the Admiralty talked round. I wonder how on earth he did it. He's some man when he gets going.'

'Look out,' Percy warned. 'I hear Gregg coming back. Good night.'

'Good night,' Timothy replied.

Over in the far corner Jackie Main had heard all that had been said, and it had left him a bit homesick. How he wished he could be one of the twelve.

What fun it would be to go up by train, help to get the schooner ready for sea, spend the days chipping, scraping, painting and storing. Then, when all was ready, they would put to sea and sail up to Inverness along the coast which he knew so well. But what was the use, he told himself. They would never pick a new boy for a job like that. Still, it was nice to imagine—and, imagining, he fell asleep to dream that he was at the helm of the *Venturer* sailing in over the Great Barrier Reef.

Chapter II

A STRANGE REQUEST

Captain Drew stood on the quayside of Darroch harbour, looking across the water at the schooner lying on the west wall. She had been a good-looking ship, and would be so again provided that the weather remained dry and let them get on with the scraping and painting. But right now she was a sorry sight. No ship looks her best without her spars and rigging, but with the iron-work rusty, the brass fittings green with the salt air and both paint and varnish work showing raw wood as well, she looked like something cast up on a desert island.

Her lines were clean, however. She would be an excellent sea boat, not fast but dependable. The previous day he had gone over her thoroughly. The copper sheathing was intact and an exhaustive scrutiny of the bilges had failed to reveal any flaw in either the planking or the timbers. Of course, the steering gear needed greasing, and the auxiliary engines were obviously ready for a thorough check-up. But these were jobs which would be done as a matter of course in the next ten days.

All the running gear would be renewed, blocks overhauled and new sails bent on. Part of the deck over the bos'n's bunk needed to be recaulked, and he had already seen the local shipbuilder and had asked him to get on with it as soon as possible.

As the Captain leant against the big crane, looking at the ship that was to be his home for the next few weeks, he thought of his own boyhood in Australia. His father had owned a ship very like the School one, and many a trip he had done on her before going to sea as an apprentice in the Radnor Line—which at that time ran ships from England to Australia, Hong Kong, Shanghai, Singapore and the Straits Settlements.

His father had been a hard taskmaster and had taught him his work well. Indeed, he still felt happier with a sailing ship beneath his feet than a steam one, even though he had his Master's ticket in both. Now here he was, about to undertake what must be one of the strangest missions ever given to an officer of the company.

When he had been sent for by the owner of the Line in Liverpool, he had had the wind up. He didn't mind admitting it. Mr Gault was a man of few words, and Drew had hardly got seated before he had been asked if he would sail the ship from Darroch to Aberdovey with a crew of twelve schoolboys and two adults, Howarth, a chief rigger from the company, and Rees, a man from Port Maddock who had also been trained in sail.

He looked at his watch, and saw that it was almost ten o'clock.

Indeed, as he moved along the water's edge, Howarth and Rees appeared beside the *Venturer*, having come down the path from the foot of Harbour Street. Howarth, a huge man, very like Hardy, of Laurel and Hardy fame, spotted him first.

'Hey, there he is,' he said, putting his kitbag on a bollard and pointing down at the figure moving towards them. 'That's 'im ; must be.

You can't mistake 'im from the description they gave us at the office. Australian, short, stocky build, very wiry, fair hair and bright blue piercing eyes—wasn't that it ? '

'Well now, I don't quite know,' replied the Welshman. 'It was you was spending all the time with the young lady, getting the instructions, I imagine.' He put his gear down beside that of his companion and added with a sly smile : 'I'm surprised you remembered it all so well. Good attention you must have been paying, man.'

Howarth turned to look at the tall, lean fellow with the big hooked nose in his blue seaman's jersey and baggy trousers. He had liked him from the first and had soon found out that life on the Port Maddock schooners had left him little or nothing to learn of sailing ships and their ways.

'Now, see here——' he began. But what he might have said was interrupted by a hail from below.

''Morning, gentlemen, and welcome to Darroch and the *Venturer*.'

They looked down to find Drew smiling up at them. A couple of bounds and he was over the rocks and shaking hands with them.

When they had introduced themselves and the Captain had enquired what the journey had been like, the three of them went aboard, down the after companion-way to the small state-room. Opening off it was the tiny cabin where Drew had got his gear partially unpacked. He showed Howarth and Rees their bunks and the small bathroom, and lifting up the charts, he swung the table up to the deckhead to expose the two twenty-horse Ailsa Craig petrol-paraffin engines.

'Wonder how much use those pieces of scrap iron will be worth in a bit of a tide?' Howarth observed.

'Shouldn't think anything, in their present state,' Drew answered him, 'and even when they are squared up they won't do more than push her round the harbour. It's all they were meant for in the first place. Anyway, I hate engines.'

'What happens through here?' Rees asked, opening the door which led for'ard.

'Oh, that? That is where the boys will sleep and eat. We'll have our grub here. They can have theirs on those tables they fit up on irons from the deckhead. You'll see them rigged tonight. Why, anything wrong? You two look as if you had seen a ghost.' Drew looked from one to the other in alarm, for indeed both men seemed to have sustained a slight shock.

It was Rees who recovered first. 'Sir,' he said. 'I'm not sure as how my hearing is quite as good as it was. Would you be good enough to repeat what you just said?'

Drew did so. The men looked even more perplexed. It was now Howarth's turn. 'Are we to understand that there are to be youngsters aboard, Captain?'

'Of course there are. That's the whole point of the exercise. You must have been told that, before you left Liverpool. This ship belongs to a school which used to be up here, St Mark's. They have been evacuated to Wales, and the ship is to be kept at Aberdovey together with the cutters and yachts which have gone down by rail. They did a lot of seamanship before the war and want to start it up again in the Dovey estuary.'

As he finished speaking Rees burst into gales of hearty laughter, while Howarth sat with his head in his hands staring at the deck.

Bit by bit the truth emerged. Neither of the men had been told what the trip was all about. They had simply had orders to proceed to Darroch and join the *Venturer*. At the office they had collected rail vouchers, a description of Captain Drew and that was all.

Howarth had let his imagination run away with him and, trading on what he took to be the top secrecy surrounding the trip, had spun his mates in the yard a wonderful tale about a new type of Q Ship with ultra-modern radar devices which he and Rees were to sail down from Scotland.

'Wouldn't be so bad if it was only the fellows in the yard, but I told the missus and all.' Howarth looked the picture of dejection. 'Just imagine what they will say when they find out we've been piloting a blooming marine kindergarten around. "What did you do in the Great War, Daddy?" Can't you hear them? I only hope they can fill their own hot water bottles, for that I won't do. Lot of enthusiastic amateurs. I always loathed week-end sailors, and now we've got ourselves a cradle full of them!'

Drew couldn't help laughing. 'Well, Mr Howarth, you should have had more sense. However, I don't think the lads will prove as useless as you fear—at least I hope not. Dr Dreaver promised me that they were a good bunch, and they will have to be, for there is a deal of work to get through and we can't do it alone. Hullo! That sounds like them now—we had better go up and see.'

From up above came the sounds of boys' voices. As the three men came on deck someone ordered :

'Ship's company—company—'shun ! '

Somewhat surprised, Captain Drew looked up at the quay to find eleven lads standing to attention, their kit laid out in front of them. As he climbed over the ship's rail the twelfth stepped smartly forward and said : 'Trenchard reporting ship's crew all present and correct, sir.'

'Thank you, Trenchard,' the Captain replied. 'Please stand them at ease.'

As Robin turned to give the order, the Captain winked at Howarth and Rees standing open-mouthed on the after deck. Addressing them he said, 'Perhaps you gentlemen would be good enough to step up here and meet the crew.'

When they had come ashore Drew spoke to the boys : 'This is Howarth, a chief rigger from the same company as I serve in Liverpool. He will be the ship's bos'n. Mr Rees, his assistant, has spent all his life in Port Maddock schooners and has the name of being one of the finest seamen on that part of the coast. My name is Captain Drew. I have been lent to the School by my shipping line to sail this vessel down. I have spent many years in this type of ship and I am thoroughly looking forward to the trip. As you will understand, there is a mighty lot to do before we can put to sea, and unless jobs are done quickly, efficiently and willingly, we will not make it. Trenchard ? '

Robin sprang to attention. 'Sir.'

'Introduce me to your crew.'

'Aye, aye, sir.'

As Robin called each name the boy came to

attention and the Captain shook hands with him' and asked where he came from, whether he was going to sea, how much sailing he had done, etc. The last in the line was Timothy Ballard. After shaking hands, the Captain picked up a model of the *Venturer* which had been precariously balanced on top of a kitbag. It was about eighteen inches long and not a bad piece of work at all.

'Where did you get this?' he asked.

'We made it, sir.'

'Made it, did you. Who is "we"?'

'All of us had something to do with it, sir.'

'Indeed, and how long did it take you?'

'Four weeks. We began it as soon as the names were posted on the board. She still needs finishing off, but she has served her purpose.'

'And what was that purpose?'

'Well, sir'—Timothy was uncomfortable—'it was Trenchard's idea. I think he could tell you better than I.'

The Captain turned to Robin and raised an eyebrow.

'We thought, sir,' said Robin in answer to the unspoken query, 'that once we got up here, time would be pretty short and that there would be a great deal to do. One or two of us could remember a bit about the *Venturer* and so, with the help of an old photograph, we got together and made this model.'

'I see. But that doesn't quite explain the purpose which your friend here says the ship has fulfilled.'

It was Robin's turn to look a bit embarrassed. 'We reckoned, sir, that you would probably be rather disappointed with being landed with a lot of

'My name is Captain Drew'

schoolboys, so we made the model and I think that each of us knows which ropes are which, what the names of all the parts are—including the sails, and we have practised putting her about, gybing, also raising and lowering the lifeboat and swinging the davits inboard and out.'

All the time he had been speaking, the Captain's steely blue eyes had never left his face. I wish he would look elsewhere, thought Robin, but he didn't and Robin continued to look straight back at him. Somehow, he felt that he was on trial before the whole crew and he knew, instinctively, that the way in which he carried it off now might well affect his whole relationship, not only with the Captain but with the bos'n and his mate as well, for the rest of the trip.

'Have you made any other preparations?' Though his gaze never faltered, the Captain's voice was not unkind.

'Yes, sir. I made out two provisional watch lists and a galley-hands' rota for the coming week.'

There was a long pause and everyone wondered what was going to happen next. Suddenly, Captain Drew smiled and patted Robin on the shoulder. 'You have done well, lad. I like your spirit—all of you. If you keep it up you will be a credit to your School. Right, fall out and get your gear stored below.'

As the boys started loading their kitbags aboard, the Captain went away to where Howarth and Rees were standing, looking a little sheepish.

'As marine kindergartens go, I should say they might do not too badly. What do you think, Mr Howarth?' he laughed.

'I grant you they are better than I expected at first sight, but I would rather wait for a day or two before saying more.'

'Ah, now it's cautious that you are, Mr Howarth,' Rees chaffed him. 'Once bitten, twice shy. Well, I say they will do all right. They are willing and if it's willing they are you can do a lot with them. I like that senior, though. He's got the makings of a good chap, indeed he has. I liked the way he stood up to you, sir. Polite he was, but quite firm.'

'I think you are right, Mr Rees. He is a lad on whom one could depend.'

As he spoke, little did Captain Drew realise how prophetic those words were to prove. Had he had but a suspicion of what lay in store he might well have given up the whole thing there and then. But he didn't and so he simply told Mr Howarth to take over, get the boys settled in and the routine under way, while he went to keep an appointment with the Met. Officer at the aerodrome of Spynie, a few miles distant.

Once he had passed the gate and had located the man he was after, his business was soon over. It was mainly of an exploratory nature. He wanted to find out all he could about the prevailing winds in the area and to get some idea from their records of the sort of weather which they might expect.

It was while he was talking to Lieut.-Commander Grice that Professor Landsberger came into the office. Even though Captain Drew had never seen the Professor before, he sensed that he was a worried man. He kept taking his glasses off and putting them on again. He continuously got up and sat down, and his hands were never still for an instant.

Grice introduced the two men and told Landsberger about Captain Drew's impending voyage. As soon as the Professor got the rough outline of the *Venturer's* trip, he suddenly became very still indeed, and questioned the Captain closely on when he expected to leave, how long he expected to take and, strangest of all, whether many people knew about the whole idea.

The Captain was very patient with him, but was a little taken aback when, on asking the Professor just why he was so interested in the *Venturer's* movements, the old fellow leapt to his feet, muttered something quite incoherent, shook hands and shuffled out of the door, remarkably quickly for one apparently so infirm.

'You don't want to pay too much attention to him,' said Grice. 'He is always a bit queer. The young pilots on the station always say he is worst at the full moon.'

Drew laughed. 'I wouldn't know, but he is certainly an odd bird. You are mainly engaged in training here, aren't you?' he went on to remark casually.

'Yes, entirely. We train bomber pilots on Airspeed Oxfords and fighter pilots on American Harvards. From time to time we have a visiting squadron up. There are some Handley Page Hampdens in just now; huge machines with an odd gun turret below the belly.'

'The Harvards are those noisy planes which make such a row on take-off, aren't they?' Drew gazed idly out of the window.

'Yes,' Grice agreed, 'they are a bit grim. They alter the pitch of their propeller once they are airborne.' He tidied his papers.

'Then what is a professor doing on a training station?' Drew had slipped the question in and had caught Grice right off his guard.

'Eh—what was that?' Taken off balance, as it were, the Lieut.-Commander hurriedly tried to compose himself again.

'I asked what a professor was doing on a training station,' Captain Drew repeated, looking very hard at Grice.

'Oh, I don't really know. He potters around at this and that. Has an office over in Q Block somewhere, I believe. But you were asking about these Harvards. Really amazing mechanism in the props. You see, to alter the pitch of the blade you . . .'

It was no good. Twice Drew tried to get the conversation back to Professor Landsberger, but Lieut.-Commander Grice would have none of it. Finally, he took his leave after making arrangements to call over for the latest report before they sailed. Odd, he thought, as he made his way over to his hired car, how fast that old man could move. There seemed to be something very fishy about him, something very fishy indeed, but he just couldn't think what.

As he was about to get into his car, he thought he heard someone call his name. He looked up in the direction of the sound, and imagined he saw a figure wave in the shadow of the porch of a brick building nearby. It only took a second to cross to the spot. But when he got there he could see no-one.

As he tried the handle of the door, it suddenly swung open, a hand seized him by his lapels and before he knew what had happened, he had been hauled into a room and the door shut behind him. As he catapulted forward, a black hood was pulled over his head and at the same time his wrists were thrust behind him and secured by a pair of handcuffs. Shaken though he was, Drew had to admit that it was a skilful piece of work.

Controlling himself as best he could, he asked : ' Perhaps now that there is no chance of my offering further resistance, you will tell me the object of this outrage ? '

' Sorry, sir—orders,' came the reply. ' If you will just come quietly it will make things a great deal easier.'

Well, it is an English voice at any rate, and for that I suppose I ought to be thankful, thought the Captain. His mind was in a whirl. I wonder what the devil it is all about.

He was being marched between two men down what seemed to be a long passage. The angle of descent was fairly steep and, so far as he could gauge, they were moving in a southerly direction.

Drew was trying to think where they were relative to buildings on the surface, when the party halted at a door. A voice bade them come in, in answer to the guard's knock. Drew was led into a room and sat down in what felt quite a comfortable chair. The voice told the guards to withdraw and, as they did so, the Captain struggled to recall where he had heard that voice before, if indeed he had ever heard it. It seemed in some odd way familiar, and yet it wasn't.

When the door had shut there was silence for a moment, broken only by the ticking of a clock. The Captain still couldn't believe that it was all true. Why, only a few hours ago he had been standing peacefully in Darroch harbour doing no-one any harm. And now where was he? Locked in some underground cavern with a time-bomb by the sound of it. The whole thing was too fantastic. It must be some kind of joke, and so far as he was concerned, a pretty poor one at that. He was about to get up when the voice spoke.

'I am sorry that it has been necessary to treat you in this cavalier fashion, Captain, and I can assure you that had any other way been open to us in the circumstances, it would not have been done. The truth is that we need your help and need it very badly.'

'Putting a hood over my head and tying my wrists like a convict is a method of approach which is not likely to secure maximum co-operation. In fact, it won't secure any at all,' rapped the Captain from the depths of the hood.

'I can understand how you feel and you will be freed just as soon as you give us your solemn oath that you will assist in every way possible and that you will not divulge anything which you may see or hear in this room.'

'Well,' gasped the prisoner, 'of all the cool cheek! I don't know where I am or who you are or what your plan is to do with me, and you have the brass neck to expect me to give my solemn word to help you! Nothing doing, gentlemen.'

'Just a moment, this is getting us nowhere,' a second voice said.

'Ah ! So there are two of you, are there ? The plot thickens,' Drew scoffed. 'Brave men indeed.'

'Now listen, Captain,' the new voice went on, 'I am the Commanding Officer of this Air Station. You are at present sitting in one of the most closely guarded rooms in the country. Its very existence is known only to a few, and the nature of the work done here is information shared by the Head of the Secret Service, Professor Landsberger and myself—no-one else.'

'So that's who owns the voice. I thought it was familiar. Please go on.'

'If you decide to help us, then the Professor and I will take you fully into our confidence. If you decline, then you will be held as a prisoner till the circumstances which have necessitated this drastic treatment have resolved themselves. I take the full responsibility for my actions in this matter. It is a question of the utmost urgency, the successful solution of which may well have a direct bearing on the conduct of the war.'

This voice carried conviction. Captain Drew made up his mind quickly. Standing up, he said : 'I am at your service and will pledge myself to do exactly as you wish.'

Immediately the hood was removed, and his hands freed. Shading his eyes from the light he saw that he was in some kind of a workshop. On a bench near him sat a rather complicated instrument made of a grey metal and equipped with numerous dials and switches. Landsberger stood with his hand on it. 'This is it,' he said. 'This is my brain child.'

His eyes accustomed to the light now, Drew

looked at him. 'Are you the fellow who was up in the Met. office ?' he asked.

The Professor laughed. 'Yes, the same, though without my simple disguise. I'm not really so old.'

'You bet you're not. You shouldn't move with such rapidity when you are impersonating an old man. You all but gave the show away, you know.'

The other was at once serious. 'I know,' he agreed. 'But you will see in a moment just how necessary it was for me to get away and find the Commanding Officer here. You were the answer to our prayers, and if you were not to slip through our fingers we had to anchor you fast. We simply couldn't risk rousing your suspicions by sending for you nor could we take a chance on anyone getting an idea of some kind of liaison between us ; hence this. Clumsy perhaps, but I hope effective.

'Briefly the position is as follows. The plans of this machine, a camera capable of photographing in all weathers both day and night up to any altitude, will be ready to go to London in ten days' time. I am doing the blueprints myself. This morning we had a coded message saying that there was reason to suppose that the Germans had got wind of my invention and that the plans should be sent by some means other than the usual channels, as enemy agents were known to have orders to stop at nothing to gain possession of them.

'Your voyage would be the perfect cover for transporting them, and once in Aberdovey, my brother, who commands the gun batteries at Towyn along the coast, would fly them to Whitehall and deliver them in person. What do you say, Drew ?'

'I'll have to get in touch with my Company and

also the Headmaster first. It's a terrific responsibility.'

'No, no; that's just what you can't do. It is much too risky. We will have to do this on our own. You see, we don't know the extent of the fifth column on the station itself. There is no-one we can safely trust.'

'Asking a tremendous lot of you, Captain,' the C.O. said, 'but you see how it is. Landsberger is right, I think. We must go it alone.'

Drew's brain raced hard. 'You leave me little alternative,' he said.

'You will do it then?'

There was a long pause.

'Yes.'

'Thank goodness. I prayed you would. You will hear from us again and we will fix the final details then. Good luck.'

Half an hour later Captain Drew was back on board the *Venturer*, having lunch and still wondering if the whole thing hadn't been some ghastly dream. That it hadn't been a hallucination was borne out by the bruise fast forming on his ankle where it had been accidentally, he hoped, hit by the guard's rifle.

Chapter III

MAKING READY FOR SEA

As soon as Captain Drew's car had gone out of sight, Howarth and Rees mustered all hands on the after end of the main deck and gave them a short, sharp introduction to life at sea, the nature of the voyage and just what would be expected of them as a crew.

Concluding the talk Howarth said, 'Now, Mr Rees and I don't mind admitting that we was a bit put out like when we 'eard as 'ow the crew was composed of nippers like yourselves. Furthermore, we 'as to admit that the seaman-like way in which you reported yourselves for dooty this morning was much to your credit. However, one swallow don't make a summer, an' don't any of you forget it. If you're on, you're on, and it don't matter wot it costs you to see the job well done. When you're off, then you can do wot you like. That right, Mr Rees?'

'Well now, I think that is all as can be said just now,' the Welshman replied, ''cept that when you are given an order you get on and obey it, whatever it may be.'

'Oh yes,' Howarth chipped in, 'I forgot that. Most important it is too. You see, if you get into the 'abit of questioning orders, then in an emergency, by the time someone 'as explained to you wot's wot, or more likely 'as cuffed you over the ear, the ship may well 'ave gone aground or something else may 'ave 'appened. All right then, fall out the galley squad and get cracking on the dinner.

The rest come round 'ere and we'll 'ave a few questions to see just wot you do know about the vessel.

'You there.' He pointed at Timothy. 'Wot's a bolt rope?'

'It's the rope sewn along the foot of a sail,' came the immediate reply.

'It is, is it?' Howarth was obviously taken aback. 'Can anyone else tell me more about it? Yes, you there with the red hair.'

'It is always on the port side in British ships, to enable you to know which way round the sail was if you were handling it in the dark.'

'Not bad, for a start. Now then, next man. Wot rope am I 'anging on to?'

'Topping lift for the fore boom, sir.'

'Good. Next one. Where would you find the gudgeons and pintles?'

'They secure the rudder to the ship, sir.'

Howarth turned to Rees with a wink. 'Would you care to have a crack at them, Mr Rees?' he asked.

Rees looked up. 'Now I wonder if any of you boys could be telling me where the dolphin-striker might be?'

'Yes, sir.' Jackie's arm shot up.

'You think you know, do you? All right, it's ready I am to hear if you can give me an answer.'

The big Welshman obviously thought that this question had stumped them. However, he hadn't reckoned with young Main. There were precious few parts of a boat which he couldn't name. Those which he didn't know by becoming conversant with them in daily trips on his father's boat during the holidays, he had learnt from the many books which he had read on seamanship in one form or another. It was while reading a book about the tea clippers that he had learnt of the dolphin-striker.

Standing up now beside the binnacle, he explained how this support projected downwards to take the stay running from the forefoot to the bowsprit. As the ship rose and fell in a seaway the end of the striker was alternately buried deep in a wave or poised high in the air.

'So you see,' Jackie finished, 'any dolphin or porpoise swimming around the stem of a ship was liable to be hit smartly over the head—hence the name, "Dolphin-striker".'

Rees came over and tousled his hair. 'Not bad at all, young 'un, and it's not out of a technical book that you read that yarn.'

While question and answer flew thick and fast on deck above, down for'ard in the galley, Trenchard got the hands going on the first meal of the boys' trip. Though not fully stored there was plenty of food both in the pantry and in the lockers. The boys soon found their way around, setting to with a will as they looked out and cleaned the pots and pans which probably had not seen the light of day since being stowed away after the last expedition, prior to the School's evacuation to Wales.

Having brought up the crew's standard of general seamanship and nautical knowledge on the way up, Robin was determined not to let the side down by bad cooking. Though not expert himself, he had a fair knowledge of camp-craft which he hoped would see him through. For this reason he had taken first spell of galley chores confident that, while he put on a meal down below, Timothy Ballard would cope with the questions of the bos'n and his mate on deck.

By the time eight bells had struck for midday all was ready. The Captain, Mr Howarth and Mr Rees ate along aft on the chart table which lowered down over the auxiliary engines, while the boys used the main saloon amidships. Two stewards took it in turns to carry the grub from the galley, which was right up for'ard over the chain locker, to the crew.

In the afternoon all hands turned to and got the sails up from the locker right aft in the very stern of the vessel. Each one was critically examined, folded and put on one side, for they were to go off that evening by lorry to the sail-maker farther down the coast where they were to be ' barked ' or dipped in tannin to preserve them. In this process they would also acquire a red colour which would look well above the black hull, white water line and varnished upper works of the ship.

It was a long, tedious job but not without interest.

After supper and a short walk around the harbour, everyone turned in early and was soon asleep. Everyone, that is, except Captain Drew. Long after the others were piped down he could be seen out on the end of the north wall by the harbour light, watching the sun go down and looking more than a little worried.

Next day work started in no uncertain fashion. By seven o'clock, when they called all hands with a cup of tea, the duty watch had coaxed the galley fire into life, had got the porridge pot boiling and had heated up sufficient water for the officers to shave and the boys to have a quick wash after their dip in the harbour. Some were still struggling into their clothes when the bos'n came roaring into the saloon like a minor typhoon.

'Now then, look nippy, you lads,' he bellowed. 'Up on deck the lot of you. Roll your trousers up and leave your socks and shoes below. Mr Rees is up for'ard with sand and brushes. He'll tell you wot to do. I want that deck as white as the driven snow in 'arf an hour. If it ain't, no breakfast—see?' And he landed Squeak Naylor a hefty crack with the flat of his enormous hand, right across his after end.

Squeak gave a yelp, bolted madly up the for'ard companion-way, tripped over the sand bucket and landed full length on the deck just as Mr Rees let drive with a bucket of water. The force behind it was considerable—it had been intended to reach the far end of the deck—so it is not surprising that it washed the hapless boy straight into the scuppers, leaving him coughing like a stranded fish.

Neil Townrow was the first to recover from the laughter which followed. He helped Squeak regain his feet on the slippery wood and saw him off below for a change of clothes.

While Robin took charge of the sanding party under Mr Rees, Timothy Ballard got the pump going and saw to it that the bilges were dry. This was a job which was carried out every morning before breakfast and last thing in the evening after supper, during the voyage. All wooden ships make a little water now and then. The *Venturer* was no exception.

After breakfast the forenoon 'jobs' were given out. There was a lot to do and very little time to do it in, but the boys enjoyed it from the start. The anchor cables were ranged along the stone wharf and three lads were put on to chip the flakes of rust off them and apply a coat of red lead. Four more, armed with paint brushes and pots, started on the paintwork aft, under the watchful eye of Mr Howarth, while at the foot of the foremast Percy Chester was coaxed into a bos'n's chair by the patient Rees.

'Now listen here, will you. I don't want to be bellowing like a bull and you in a stiff breeze at the masthead,' he said. Percy's complexion went from white to green. 'You know what you 'ave to do. Rub the mast all round with the sandpaper, wipe it well with the cloth and then varnish it. When you have done all you can reach, give a yell and we'll lower you a bit.'

Chester had often wondered what space flight would be like. He got a rough idea when the Welshman laid hands on the rope fall and started to heave. In no time he had been hoisted from the deck and left dangling like a daddy-longlegs beneath a block on the cross trees. By the time he had recovered his breath and ventured to look down, Mr Rees had made him fast and was already issuing orders for another job.

There was nothing for it but to get to work, sandpapering the mast before giving it a liberal coat of varnish. Percy did his best and for a while all went well. But luck was against him that day, for no sooner had he, on one occasion, dipped his brush into the pot than a huge gull glided close to his head to alight on the spar above him. How graceful it looked, he thought; how wonderfully white its feathers, and how black its eyes. Lost in admiration, he sat swinging his arm idly to and fro, oblivious of the consternation which his action was causing on deck below.

At about the same time at which Percy started thinking of the bird, Captain Drew came on deck from his cabin, where he had been correcting charts and studying the North Sea Pilot. Blinded for a moment by the bright sun he stood shading his eyes from the glare, looking over the side at a seine-net boat which had just come in.

Suddenly he started to feel his shirt all over as a fine spray came down from a cloudless sky. Next instant he darted under cover of the port lifeboat, roaring at the unfortunate Percy to pay attention to what he was doing. But his words were never heard at the masthead where the miscreant sat, a steady stream of varnish flowing from his brush, which the breeze whipped aft and dropped as a gentle, sticky rain everywhere.

In the end the situation was brought under control by the presence of mind of Trenchard, who quickly cast off the halyard and lowered Chester smartly on to the deck, where he was dressed-down in no uncertain manner by the irate skipper. Half an hour later, when he had cleaned off the mess, he was back at the masthead, chastened and determined to keep his mind on his work this time.

As soon as it was low water, everyone stopped whatever he was doing, put on sea boots and started to dig the sand away from round the keel. Through rising and falling for so long with each tide, the *Venturer* had dug for herself a deep trench in the harbour bottom. Before she could be got out the boys had to clear away the obstruction, thus connecting her self-made lock with the deep water beyond. It was an unpleasant job ; hard and grim among the slime and filth of the mud. The heat made the stench almost unbearable.

So it went on for the following ten days. No sooner was one job finished than another had to be begun. There was ballast to shift—great blocks of pig-iron below the deck boards in the saloon ; new life-saving gear checked and stowed, to conform with Board of Trade regulations ; all the cordage was replaced and the blocks greased and overhauled. ‘ Dod, the Engineer ’—he was never known as anything else—serviced the windlass, the two auxiliary engines and ‘ Macbeth ’, the small electrical generator housed beside the steering box on deck. The machine derived its name from the fact that, when running, it effectively ‘ murdered sleep ’.

In the early evening, when the fishing boats had finished using it, the *Venturer*'s crew had the use of the one and only water tap which Darroch harbour boasted. It was as far away from the vessel as it could be, so the only way to fill the fresh-water tanks was by a human chain and bucket system.

During all the hard work, the dirt and the noise, Robin Trenchard proved himself to be a born leader. No matter what the task or how unpleasant it promised to be, he was always the first to volunteer. So infectious was his enthusiasm that he kept everyone in high spirits with his good-natured fun and ready wit. The boys almost worshipped him, and the officers very soon came to respect him as a sound, hard-working lad who would never turn in a shoddy piece of work or for that matter let anyone else do so if he could possibly prevent it. Captain Drew was impressed by him—so much so that on more than one occasion he gave serious thought to an idea which, on first sight, seemed too dangerous for words. However, the more he saw of the boy, the more he felt that he could trust him when the time came.

At last, the toil and energy so willingly given began to show results. *Venturer*, glowing in her new paint, her running rigging gleaming white, was almost ready for sea. In two days' time she would sail on the spring tide out into the Moray Firth, through the Narrows at Fort George and so on up to Inverness on the first leg of the course to Aberdovey.

As excitement grew among the boys, so did Captain Drew's apprehension increase. He had heard no more from Professor Landsberger or the C.O. of Spynie. Indeed, the whole incident could well have been a bad dream but for the reminder, in the form of a large, tender area on his ankle, now slowly changing from blue to yellow. It had been a painful bruise.

Sitting late that night in his cabin checking the various courses, the Captain lit his pipe as he sat back for a moment going over the peculiar events which had happened since he took command of the sailing ship. His mind worked backwards and forwards studying the problem from every angle, but at about one o'clock in the morning he gave it up and prepared to turn in. As he folded the charts he thought, 'I wonder just how or when I shall hear from these fellows again?'

The answer came almost at once, as if in direct reply to his unspoken question. There was a rustle in the pipe over his head which connected with the squat mushroom ventilator on deck, as a slip of pink paper fluttered down. Quickly unfolding it, he read the cryptic message : *Primrose, 12,00.00.*

In a couple of bounds he was out of his cabin and up the after companion-way. There was no-one to be seen on deck. The night was still and hot, the tide almost full. Not a soul moved ashore. As he peered round, his eye caught the shine of the moon on wet planking. He looked closer. Yes, there it was, the mark where someone had climbed out of the water and up over the ship's side.

Captain Drew stood baffled. His visitor might have come that way, but how did he depart ? The moon, now nearly full, cast its light straight across the water. Anyone swimming would have been clearly visible. He was still wondering when he thought he heard the low throb of a boat's engine off the harbour mouth. He jumped ashore and softly sprinted down to the west wall. Standing listening, he heard it again, the sound of an engine, hardly turning over as it slid away into the darkness.

It was not till he was shaving next morning that the truth dawned on him. Suddenly, he understood it all ; the water, the absence of a swimmer, the boat off the entrance and the strange, ribbed, triangular mark on deck in the moonlight.

Chapter IV

NO TURNING BACK

There was only one full day left before the *Venturer* sailed, and it promised to be a really hard one. The stores were due to start arriving at the quayside at eight o'clock. Before they had finished the crew would have handled everything from tins of fruit, salt beef and sail twine, to a spare anchor, galley coal and a new chronometer.

They were up early, squaring off their bunks, also the breakfast dishes, long before the first lorry arrived. When it did grind to a halt alongside the ship's rail, the boys were all ready for work, having been briefed by Trenchard in exactly what was wanted.

Just before they began lifting the boxes, someone told Percy to nip ashore to the ship chandler's at the far side of the harbour, to see if he could get hold of some green paraffin for the starboard light. There was about half a gallon of red oil in the paint store which would do the port lamp, they said, but the green tin was getting low.

Obediently, Chester heaved himself up over the rail on to the quay to wander off, humming quietly and giving no sign at all that he had noticed the winks or suppressed sniggers which accompanied his departure. Even the bos'n allowed himself a broad grin at this naïve display on the part of the ship's comic.

While the work of storing went on, Captain Drew walked round to the old tarred shed where

Dod had his cubby-hole. He wanted to have a word with him about the accumulators for the transmitter, but he also hoped to find out something which would solve the message on the pink slip of paper.

'12' seemed obvious—today was the 12th. '00.00' he took to mean midnight. But 'Primrose'—that had him squarely stumped. Might be the name of a house, a hotel or even one of the other ships in the harbour, he thought. On the other hand it could also refer to a person of that name who lived in Darroch and whom he was supposed to contact at the time indicated. The possibilities appeared endless, but the time left for solving them was short.

After deciding that two of the batteries should be renewed and the remainder serviced, the Captain started to chat to the electrician about local customs, names and places. He was glad of a break in the morning's work and was only too pleased to gossip with the skipper.

But though Drew learnt much of the history, the background and even a good deal of the inhabitants' private lives, he failed to get the faintest hint of that for which he sought. Ask outright, he dare not, for if he had learnt only one thing it was this, that the whole affair was in deadly earnest, and by no slip, however small, must he chance a 'leak' to the enemy.

He was just turning to leave the shed when he noticed a small block of stone lying inside the door. It was rough sandstone, much like any other piece of local stone, but what caught the Captain's eye was what looked like an animal carved on one side of it. The image was faint but by moving it so as to reflect the light at a certain angle, it showed up unmistakably.

'Odd-looking thing,' he said to Dod. 'Find it hereabouts?'

'Yes, got it one day up on the beach at Primrose Bay, just below the cliff.'

Drew froze solid, while peculiar flutters, like those one gets before the start of a rugger match, ran round inside his tummy. Controlling his voice with a great effort, he asked the other all about it, and how he came to spot this particular piece. His joy was unbounded when he learnt in the course of the conversation that there was a cave in the rock, decorated with many of these examples of prehistoric art and that a stone jetty ran seawards for a short distance marking the site of a very old harbour. It was difficult, Dod said, to get down on to the beach because the sides of the cave were precipitous where stone had been quarried and shipped away many years ago.

So that's it, the Captain thought as he puffed at his pipe on the way back to *Venturer*—twelve o'clock tonight at the cave in Primrose Bay. Well, I wonder what will happen next!

Lunchtime came and went, but still the stores kept arriving. Mr Howarth, assisted by Mr Rees, checked each item, great and small, before appointing it to its specific place for stowage for the journey. By six o'clock the last spare coils of rope had been heaved aboard. With a sigh as he wiped the sweat from his brow, Mr Howarth gave the order.

'Clew up, lads, we'll call it a day.'

No-one was sorry to hear him speak; they were all exhausted.

Ballard was up by the windlass squaring off the headsails and staysail sheets. The ropes had been used to help get gear on deck and now he was making them up neatly, putting them back on their belaying pins. He looked up towards the town, but could hardly believe what he saw. There, wandering down towards the ship was Chester, hands clean, hair brushed, looking fresh as a daisy.

He came on to the ship and made his way aft to where Howarth was having a word with the Captain.

'Well, lad, what is it?' Drew asked half over his shoulder.

'Beg to report that I have been unable to secure any green oil, sir.'

'Oh, very well then.' The skipper turned away, then suddenly spun round: 'Green oil, Chester—*what* green oil?' he snapped.

Percy looked the picture of innocence.

'For the starboard light, sir. I was sent for it.'

'Yes, man,' thundered the Captain, 'but that was at eight this morning.'

'That's correct, sir. I have tried everywhere. I even walked to the other village along the coast to try there.'

'Well now, if that don't cap the lot.' Mr Howarth was almost speechless. 'In my time I've seen them pretty raw, but this is the limit. Where did you get your lunch?'

'I had a snack in the hotel, sir.'

'Very nice too,' commented the Captain, 'and you missed all the work into the bargain. Go on! Get below and give a hand in the galley.'

It was just as well for Percy that only Ballard

saw him give a broad wink, putting his fingers to his lips as he slid down the companion-way !

Green oil, my foot, thought Timothy, he knew all the time there was no such thing. He's all there that lad, every inch of him.

Night fell, the ship became still as all hands got to bed early, tired after the strenuous day. Before very long the only sound was the gentle creaking of the fenders as they rubbed between the ship and the stonework. Captain Drew had told Mr Howarth that he was having a meal ashore with friends, and that he should turn in himself when he felt like it.

By twenty minutes to twelve he was on the cliff-head above Primrose Bay, some two miles east of Darroch. It had not been an easy journey for him because he had taken stringent precautions to see that no-one should have the opportunity of following him.

As he approached the area, moving carefully among the whins he saw a very new notice proclaiming that the place was being used as a War Office range, and therefore liable to danger from unexploded bombs. The paint glistened in the eerie light. For a moment he paused. Something was worrying him. Then he had it—the smell of paint, that was it, overpowering in the evening air. Drew retraced a few steps to examine the board more closely. To his astonishment the paint was quite wet when he touched it.

Far below him the waves broke on the old jetty in endless succession, but though the swell was moderate, the noise was magnified by the surrounding wall of rock into a frightening roar. Very slowly he picked his way down the narrow path, a track which at times was no more than a foot wide, wedged between the dripping, slimy rocks and the sheer drop to the stones beneath.

As he descended deeper, the sound increased, till it filled the air. Coming from every direction, battering the ear-drums with incessant crescendo, it had some evil foreboding which seemed to foretell disaster. While rounding a particularly difficult bend he was suddenly struck a terrific blow on the nape of his neck. Burning pain seared through his flesh and he heard a piercing scream above the thunder of the sea.

In his fright Captain Drew flung himself into a shallow niche, and as he lay there with pounding heart he heard what sounded like a boulder bouncing down from the path above, as though loosened by a careless foot. He listened again, but all was silence except the sea's pounding on the old jetty stanchions.

Suddenly, just beside his head there was a tremendous commotion. In the half light—for it is never really dark in summer in those latitudes—he sensed, rather than saw, a white bullet rocket out, far out over the dark waters. He knew then what it was that had hit him—a sea bird, scared by his presence had flown out from the cliff face, inadvertently striking him as it did so.

Staunching the blood as best he could, Captain Drew carried on down towards the low, grassy knoll leading up to the cave. On the stroke of midnight he took up his position just inside the narrow entrance. Dank, fetid air filled his nostrils.

As he stood waiting, the silent seconds slipping past, the skipper could not help thinking of the odd stories which Dod had recounted ; how a secret passage was supposed to go straight inland from this cave to come up in the centre of the peculiarly constructed steading of Ogston House.

And then there was the time when customs men had raided the cave in search of contraband, but the smugglers had been informed and, being ready, had chopped off their heads as they bent low to enter. In order to dispose of the bodies, so the story went, they had. . . .

Drew's thoughts suddenly stopped, the veins in his body tingled, he felt as if the hair was rising on the back of his head. Out of the dark waters beside the pier two hideous objects were emerging slowly, ponderously. The shapes were human by suggestion, but there the similarity ended. Each was covered in dark, shiny black skin which had at one extremity a pair of long webbed feet, and at the other a head of the same substance with an oval, cyclop's eye. Their gait as they advanced up the causeway was heavy beneath their monstrously hunched shoulders. The light played strange tricks, but even allowing for that, both creatures seemed to be over six feet in height.

On they came, their wet feet making an odd slosh-slosh noise. For a second the moon shone clearly down upon them and in that instant two things happened. First, the Captain recovered his habitual coolness of mind ; secondly, as he recognised the apparitions for what they were—frogmen in the latest diving equipment—a shadow detached itself from the darkness to hurl full at the knees of the second man, bringing him down in a superb rugby tackle.

Looking back, Drew was never really sure of

what happened next. His only clear recollection was of having his arms pinioned from behind, while something pushed past him to join the fight on the beach. In a few moments it was all over. Drew with the attacker, his head bound in a bag, was now back in the cave with the frogmen. Whoever it was that had materialized from the depths of the cave to tie him up, had been left on guard outside the entrance now closed up by layers of sacking.

The underwater men had taken off their helmets and cylinders. Switching on their torches they enabled the Captain to recognise Professor Landsberger and the Commanding Officer of Spynie. Both were armed.

'Well, well,' said Drew to the Professor. 'Now that we three have met again—what next?'

'Cut it out, Captain'—the voice was almost a snarl. 'You have to explain this doublecross away first.'

'Doublecross—I don't follow you, Landsberger.'

'Your plan was good, but mine was better,' came the reply. 'You and your accomplice were to deal with the Commanding Officer and myself encumbered with our heavy equipment. But you did not know, poor fool, that your every movement has been tracked since you left your ship in Darroch. As you came along the cliff you passed through a ring of my men who reported your progress by wireless. The notice roused your curiosity by its wet paint. That was an afterthought to keep away any possible strangers who might chance to go that way.' He paused, looking at Drew.

'You know, sir, I would have been prepared to trust him anywhere, last time we met.'

'Yes,' replied the C.O. 'Just how wrong can one be?' He was nursing a damaged knee and a badly bruised thigh.

'If it hadn't been for my men hidden at the rear of the cave we should have been done for and your plans would have been gone.'

'Now just one moment, you two.' Drew cut in with some asperity, 'I am sick of you and your fairy tales. You are a couple of melodramatic idiots. So far as I am concerned you can take yourselves and your plans out to Davy Jones—and stay there. I came here at considerable personal inconvenience to help you with a scheme which you persuaded me was worth-while, being of vital interest in the conduct of the war. Since meeting you I have had nothing but abuse and rough handling from your minions. Now stop playing at robbers and Indians and get out of here.'

There was a movement from the hooded figure in the corner. It groaned as it turned over, regaining consciousness.

'Not so fast with your well simulated indignation, Captain Drew.' Landsberger's voice was deadly cold as his blue eyes looked steadily down the barrel of an automatic. 'We are to take it that you disown this man; that he is not in league with you?' he continued in chilling, measured tones.

'Of course, of course.' Drew was growing more impatient.

During the conversation the C.O. had unobtrusively loosened the knots round the sack. Quickly whipping off the covering, he barked at the skipper: 'Then how do you account for this ?' As he spoke he shone his torch full upon the deathly white face of—Robin Trenchard.

Drew gasped and started forward to tend the wound on the head from which the blood seeped down to matt with the hair above the collar. In a flash Landsberger was between them, motioning him back with his gun.

'So you do know him,' he sneered. 'I thought perhaps you would. No—don't get excited, he is not badly hurt,' he went on as the other again made to come forward. 'In a moment or two he will talk.'

And talk Robin did, a second or two later as the Captain was going for Landsberger and the C.O., calling them everything to which he could lay his tongue. When Robin had recovered sufficiently to give a coherent account of himself, even Drew could scarcely believe his ears.

Robin had been wakened the previous night by the sound of the frogman surfacing and climbing on deck alongside the porthole by his bunk. He had lain awake, trying to puzzle out the reason for the noise, but thought that he had dozed off again, only to be re-awakened by the click of the Captain's cabin door shutting.

Well roused this time, he had gone above, silently ; had seen the flipper mark on the wet deck and, through a chink in the skylight curtains, had seen Drew reading the pink slip. Unable to make head or tail of what was happening he decided to follow the skipper everywhere he went, certain that sooner or later he would be needed.

'And so,' he concluded, 'here I am. I knew the Captain was in the cave, alone as I thought. Seeing two of you advancing and up to no good, I reckoned that if I tackled one, it would give the skipper a chance to surprise the other.'

The two Servicemen took a lot of persuading, but finally accepted the account of the night's proceedings.

Being now so far in the know, Robin was solemnly sworn to secrecy and put in the picture with regard to the real object of the present meeting. Though his head ached and pounded, he was thrilled by the confidence now placed in him, especially when Captain Drew revealed that he had intended using him to guard the plans anyway, though without revealing their confidential nature.

Time was running on and the tide, now well on the turn, would shortly give rise to dangerous currents around the point if the swimmers did not get away at once. The C.O. felt well enough to make the trip to the boat, though Robin's flying tackle had shaken him up considerably.

The plans were handed over and with a final wave the two men disappeared below the water as mysteriously as they had come.

Chapter V

WORKING UP SHIP

Venturer plunged her stem deep into the trough of a wave while the spray flew up over the rail to be whipped off by a moderately strong breeze blowing from the east on her starboard bow.

When the ship rose on the next crest there came a deafening crash amidships, accompanied by a howl as Chester went headlong into the scuppers, followed by a huge basin of potatoes which he had been preparing for lunch. Before he could gather his scattered wits, they had shipped another green 'un which flowed round the mast and deck gear to add its volume to that already sloshing around his prostrate form.

Rees roared with laughter, surveying the scene from the shelter of the for'ard companion-way.

'I told you not to sit there, man, didn't I now, an' I warned you last night that you would find cooking at sea a darned sight more difficult than when she was sitting on the mud in Darroch harbour. But it's the hard way you have chosen and now you know.'

He went below, still chuckling, leaving Percy to make good the damage as best he could.

Poor Percy, he was having a rough time of it, and had been ever since they set sail early that morning. As they left the quay, all hands were on duty, first to clear the entrance, and then to make sail. Though they all knew what to do in theory, and in spite of having practised in port, they found the job of hoisting the canvas infinitely more difficult with the deck canted well over in one direction as it heaved up and down. Furthermore, the motion hadn't done his tummy any good at all. When the four-hour watches had been set he had been ready to coil up on his bunk. It was only as he made to go below that the sight of the port watch going off reminded him that it was his trick on deck—and he was to report to the galley.

Now, soaked to the skin, he had to admit that the sudden accident had banished his illness though at a greater cost to his comfort and dignity than he was willing to pay. Carefully, he retrieved the last potato, putting it back into the basin, and as he did so, Mr Howarth, on watch beside the man on the wheel, sang out :

'Stand by to lower inner and outer head sails.'

Being one of the crew detailed for this job, Percy sprinted for'ard as best he could with the deck heaving beneath him. Up in the fore part he was joined by Jackie Main who deftly cast off the outer jib halyard calling on Chester to pull away on the down haul as he did so.

For two or three fathoms the rope ran cleanly through the sheave but suddenly it stuck fast. Nothing which the two boys could do was of any use in freeing it. Hoist and lower as they might, the sail refused to come down.

'Don't stand looking at it, boy. Get out to the end of the bowsprit and clear it. Look nippy too. I can't keep her up in the wind for ever.'

Venturer was losing way, her sails flapping, as Howarth kept her heading into the breeze in order to take pressure off the canvas.

'What's wrong with you, Chester, didn't you

'ear me the first time? Get yourself outboard and see to it.'

Percy looked ahead to the end of the spar with the stay beneath, now poised high above the crested seas, now dipping down to skim over their foaming tops and separated from them by little more than a coat of varnish.

Since being put in charge of the head sails, he had dreaded this emergency, knowing that in all probability it would come, but fearful that when it did his nerve would fail him at the crucial time. *Venturer* had no safety net below the bowsprit. One slip——

'Off you go, Percy. I'll give you a hand. Jackie, stand by the ropes.'

Unseen by the other two, Trenchard had come up from amidships.

'Bad block, I'm afraid, sir,' he called aft to the bos'n. 'Take two of us on it.'

The ship hauled herself up over an extra heavy sea to slide with alarming speed into the succeeding trough. As she careered downwards Percy remembered a trip on the Giant Dipper at Blackpool, and how his tummy had felt then. When it seemed that nothing could save them from total immersion in the cold waters of the Moray Firth he closed his eyes terrified, waiting for the end.

There was a jerk on the stay which caused him to lose his foothold. Instinctively he clutched the solid wood beneath his chest as the vessel rushed upwards over the next wall of foam. For a second her bow seemed to hang, poised between sea and sky before starting the sickening plunge. This time, however, a smaller wave had slid beneath her.

The fore foot smashed down with the noise of a giant ice-crusher, sending white billows of froth cascading away on either side of her stem, and a shudder through the ship which made her timbers shake from truck to keel. As though stunned by the blow, the schooner sailed on an even keel for the following seconds, gathering her strength to begin the cycle again.

Measured in time the two boys had been on the job for a matter of minutes but in that span the younger lad had known the real meaning of fear. He was frightened as never before in his life. Rolling in off the starboard bow another sea could be seen bearing down on them.

His feelings clearly written on his face, Percy turned to Robin to confess that he could not go on, that he must go back to the safety of the deck again. But the words choked in his throat as Robin put his mouth close to the youngster's ear.

'Terrific fun, isn't it? It's the nearest thing to flying on a ship.' He bawled, 'Look! Here's another coming. Bend your knees to take the jerk as she comes out of the trough—not so much chance of being shaken off. Watch it—we're off.'

With horror Chester saw that the Head of School was enjoying the experience as the bowsprit rose higher and higher into the air. He tossed the hair back from his eyes and started to hum a tune.

Between the more violent actions they were able to inch their way out towards the block, and after some difficulty, cleared it. They then sat there for a little while, not by Percy's choosing, but because Robin was on the inboard end in no hurry to get back.

Howarth had let her fall off the wind. Gathering speed, the ship fairly hurled herself at the breakers. To his astonishment Percy found himself caught up in Robin's enthusiasm, and actually enjoying it. He was sorry in a way when they were aft again reporting to the bos'n.

'Well done, you two. Not an easy job, or a pleasant one. Off you go.'

It was a laconic greeting but from Howarth it represented high praise indeed. Percy wanted to thank Robin but didn't quite know how to begin. He was, however, saved from embarrassment when the older boy patted him on the shoulder.

'Well done, Chester,' he said. 'Everyone has to do it the first time, and we're all a bit scared. You'll enjoy it the next time, though. Cheerio.'

Percy had a funny feeling in his throat, but before he could think of anything to say, Trenchard was away.

All morning the bos'n and his mate kept the boys hard at it.

Squeak Naylor was getting the weather forecast on the ship's receiver when Jackie came into the tiny wireless room.

'Hullo,' he said. 'Seen Trenchard's head?'

'No,' replied Squeak. 'What's wrong with it?'

'I was up for'ard putting her about when I noticed a patch of plaster in his hair,' Jackie went on. 'Looked bad and I asked him how it had happened. He said that he had banged it coming up out of the fore hatch this morning. No-one seems to have seen it happen, but he's looking a bit white all the same.'

'Teach him to keep his big head low in future.

Now pipe down, there's a good chap, while I take this gen for the old man.'

In the Captain's cabin Trenchard stood before the skipper, feet apart, hands behind his back.

'I gave you permission to go about today so long as you did nothing strenuous, Trenchard. Going on deck, what do I find but you and Chester on the bowsprit. How do you explain it? Couldn't he have done the job himself, whatever it was?'

'Well, not really, sir. It required both of us. The block for the outer downhaul was badly jammed and the way in which the ship was pitching made it rather difficult for one person to set it free.'

Robin felt most uncomfortable. He had been given strict orders not to do too much. In fact, it was on this clear understanding that he had escaped being confined to his bunk for the day. His head ached but he felt that if he kept going fewer questions would be asked. Anyway, he was needed about the deck while Mr Howarth, with his able assistant Mr Rees, was putting the boys through their paces in 'Working up ship'. His excuse, he knew, was weak. Moreover, Captain Drew was not a man accustomed to having his orders disobeyed.

As he had expected, he got a good dressing-down for what he had done. That over, the Captain told him to sit down while he carefully explained a plan which, he said, had first occurred to him several days prior to the incident at Primrose Bay.

Briefly, it was this. Trenchard should wear the plans strapped to his body in a form of watertight canvas belt; the idea being that no-one would be likely to suspect that they were not in the possession of the skipper himself. Any attack or difficulty would be directed against Drew should the enemy by any chance find that the documents were aboard the *Venturer*.

Robin readily agreed to wear the belt, though he was not a little afraid of the responsibility which its acceptance laid upon him.

That the game was a dangerous one he already knew, and as he bound the green canvas about his waist, he had a strange feeling that many unforeseen things might happen before he shed it again. The Captain shook hands with him, wished him luck and went on deck.

Seeing him free, Howarth and Rees converged on him.

'I think as 'ow the lads have had enough for the time being.' Howarth wiped his dirty hands on some cotton waste. 'An' right well they've done,' he continued. 'I take back my earlier doubts. When I seen them going up one side of the main-mast rigging over the table an' down the other with the ship pitching and rolling like she was tormented, I knew we 'ad lads o' the right metal. What do you think, Mr Rees?'

The Welshman looked up. 'Well now, boy, it's a long time since I saw a kinder act than Robin taking young Chester out on the boom this morning. 'E did just the right thing and at the right time. Indeed to goodness if he hadn't acted quick like he did, the young 'un's nerve would have gone, for he was pretty scared.'

'So that's it,' said Drew. 'He mothered old Chester and then took the row himself. Well, well. He never gave me the slightest inclination of how the wind stood.'

Rees smiled. ' You would hardly be expecting him to, now would you, sir ? '

' No,' the skipper replied. ' It's the last thing he would have done.'

The early afternoon saw *Venturer* past the Spits of Cromarty, running free with the wind right aft, making good way through the south channel towards the narrows at Fort George. Before rounding Chanonry Point, they took the sail off her and started the auxiliaries, for her draught was such that she had to use the tortuous deep water course which wound about under the lee of the Black Isle, rather than run straight up the firth to Inverness and the entrance to the Caledonian Canal.

Each boy had been given a spell on the wheel so that he could get used to the helm orders. As they closed the sea lock at Clachnaharry it was Neil Townrow's trick.

The bos'n was up for'ard, attending to the head ropes. Mr Rees was amidships squaring off the sails, putting on the gaskets and looking out the fenders. Aft, Captain Drew conned the ship from his stance midway between the wheel and the after companion-way at the foot of which crouched Robin Trenchard with his companion, Timothy Ballard, nursing the two thirty-horse-power Ailsa Craig petrol-paraffin engines.

' Port easy.'

' Port easy, sir,' came the reply.

' More port.'

' More port, sir.'

' Steady as you go.'

' Steady, sir.'

Neil spun the wheel quickly to starboard to meet the swing of the ship's head.

' Half ahead two.'

' Half ahead two, sir.'

As the throttles were eased back, both engines slowed down. Robin bellowed to Timothy above the din.

' Don't like the sound of this pair at all.'

' Neither do I, but don't you think that Aggie sounds less healthy than Theresa ? ' he called, using the names by which the machines were affectionately known.

' Slow ahead two.'

' Slow ahead two, sir.'

The throttles were eased back farther.

' Starboard easy.'

' Easy starboard, sir.'

' Steady.'

' Steady, sir.'

The schooner glided towards the first lock gate.

' Stop both.'

' Stop both, sir.'

The engines raced a little as the boys eased both clutches out. Cautiously they closed the throttles.

Suddenly Timothy's engine, Aggie, made a despairing gargling noise, sighed gently and was still. It happened in an instant leaving the ship without power on her starboard screw. Ballard quickly put in the impulse starter, engaged the handle, after putting her on to petrol, and swung the heavy engine. He tried several times but to no avail. Each time he turned her over there were the most awful watery noises from the direction of the cylinders.

The bowsprit rose gently over the lock gate

On deck, the bowsprit was approaching the far lock gate. The lock-master signalled the Captain to ease up.

'Slow astern two.'

'Starboard engine dead. Slow astern port, sir,' Robin called up the companion-way.

'I said slow astern two—not port, Trenchard. Pay attention will you?'

'Yes, sir, but——'

'Half astern two.'

The bowsprit was reaching out towards the gate and closing with it far too quickly for the shore gang's peace of mind. They made frantic signals now.

'Full astern two, quickly.'

In desperation Robin gave Theresa full revs astern.

'Port engine full astern!' he shouted.

Obviously the Captain didn't realise what had happened and Timothy left his efforts to try to explain. As he leapt up on deck, the bowsprit rose gently up over the lock gate, was halted by the stay carrying the dolphin-striker, paused for a moment and then slipped back ever so slowly.

As it did so, pandemonium broke loose. The shore crew blamed the bos'n who shouted back at them. The lock-master came tearing aft to Drew shaking his fist, his face almost puce with rage. Drew bellowed at the engineers, demanding to know why they had stalled the engines.

In a long, black car on the road nearby, the scene was being watched by three men in dark suits.

CHAPTER VI

RUNNING REPAIRS

THERE was nothing for it but to put ropes ashore and work the vessel by hand, together with the one sound engine. By careful management they got her through both the sea lock and the one following, up into the basin at Muirtown where she was to make fast for the night. Once there, the duty hands set to preparing the evening meal.

During the sail the compass had been giving the various boys on the wheel quite a bit of trouble. Though supposed to have been overhauled in Darroch it had developed a bubble, with the result that it was difficult to see the lubber line. It was hard enough to keep this mark on the bowl, representing the ship's head, in line with the course to be steered on the card at the best of times: the largish spherical bubble, bobbing from side to side made it nearly impossible. The course was obvious; the remedy simple—or so it seemed. Air had got into the alcohol which filled the bowl and damped the swing of the card. Squeak was sent ashore to get some more and told to top it up.

While the meal was in course of preparation all hands set about making up the sails. The canvas was hauled out taut off the booms from below before being thrown over inside itself and rolled up to form a tight skin. When it had been done according to Mr Howarth's satisfaction he gave the order 'On gaskets' and the short lengths of rope were passed over sails and spars before being securely knotted.

Up in the forepart Mr Rees was hard at it with a squad, getting the ropes neatly coiled up on the belaying pins in order to clear the decks for a quick scrub down. Along the quayside a small knot of spectators stood idly watching as the boys got everything squared off for the night.

Captain Drew had gone ashore to the Caledonian Canal offices as soon as the lines were fast to attend to the ship's papers and the dues for the passage. He had been away for about half an hour or so and on his return had gone straight below to his room. On entering it he was astounded to see his desk open, also the linen of his bunk disturbed. He sent immediately for Robin.

'Have you been aboard since we docked?' he asked when Trenchard reported.

'Yes, sir, all the time.'

'Have the bos'n and his mate been here as well?'

'Yes, sir. Mr Howarth has been aft and Mr Rees for'ard. I have been going between them all the time getting gear stowed. Anything wrong, sir?'

'My room has been searched.' Drew saw no point in beating about the bush.

'Searched?' Robin exclaimed. 'How—by whom—when?' He looked quite shaken. 'Shall I nip up and see if anyone is about the shore side?'

'No. That would do little good. He won't be hanging about, whoever it was. I know when it was done—during the past half hour—but by whom and by what means he got on board remains to be seen.'

There was a knock at the cabin door and Mr Howarth poked his head in.

'Beggin' your pardon, sir, but I just popped

down to see as 'ow you'd got your parcel. But I see you have it there on the settee all right,' he added, indicating a rectangular package which up till then had escaped the Captain's notice.

'Thanks, bos'n. When did it arrive?'

'Just after you'd gone ashore, sir. Funny-looking bloke brought it. Didn't take to 'im myself, but he did say as how he came from the ship chandler's. Be off on deck now, sir.'

He climbed back aloft. Drew stiffened.

'I ordered nothing ashore,' he said ominously. 'Here, let me open it. Bos'n must have told him to put it in.'

He quickly undid the coarse string to reveal a brick, wrapped in several sheets of brown paper. There was an uneasy silence as the two faced each other across the table.

'They haven't waited long,' the Captain said softly.

'No,' Robin agreed, 'and they seem to know what they are after. What will you do, sir, go to the police'?

'That is out of the question. You see, the extent of the fifth column is not fully known. Landsberger made me promise to see this through to Aberdovey alone. I wonder if he knew what he was asking of us.' As he spoke Drew slowly lit his pipe.

Suddenly he said: 'You had better let me have those plans back, Robin.'

'But, sir——'

'Don't argue. Give them to me quickly. This thing begins to look nasty and we have no right to involve you in what may follow.'

'May I say something before I hand them back, sir?' Robin asked.

'Yes, if you are quick about it.' The Captain looked uneasy.

'It looks as if they suspect that the plans are on board,' Robin began.

'Obviously.'

'If they don't find them on the ship, then they will think that you carry them on you, sir.'

'Well?'

Robin paused. He didn't quite know how to continue. Finally he blurted out: 'They may attack you, sir.'

'Yes, I had thought of that.' Drew's gaze was quite steady as he looked at the boy.

'But it is vital that the plans go through, sir, isn't it?'

'Of course.'

'Then if you take them back you will play straight into their hands. It would be far more sensible to leave them with me, then we can keep an eye on each other.'

In his excitement, Robin had leaned across the table and had so far forgotten himself as to pound his fist under the Captain's nose. He quickly recovered, apologising for his bad manners, and in doing so, turned towards the door.

'Don't go. I know exactly how you feel, lad; and respect you for it. But this is war, and I have a duty towards your parents. These men are desperate. They may even kill.' His last words were said slowly, with emphasis, as he looked at the youngster.

Robin Trenchard stood erect. 'I understand that, sir. In a few months I shall be at sea. Things are not easy in the Merchant Service just now and

I am no longer a child. I know what lies ahead. Please let me help you in this task. I promise not to let you down.'

The silence which followed in the small cabin was broken only by the ticking of the chronometers. Up on deck a voice from the galley called : ' Come and get it ! '

After what seemed an eternity the Captain rose, knocking the ash from his pipe as he did so.

' There is something in what you say, Robin, though I am sorry you were let in for it at all. You are right in that it will take both of us all our time to cope. We cannot, dare not, trust another soul. Set the ship on double watches night and day—four hours on ; four off. Send Mr Howarth and Mr Rees to me. I will tell them that someone has been in my room but that he must have been disturbed before he stole anything. This will account for our security in letting no-one aboard without my personal permission. Off you go to the saloon.'

Feeling a sense of relief mingled with excitement, Robin climbed the companion-way to the after deck where he gave Mr Howarth the Captain's message. On receiving it that worthy was none too pleased, but an order was an order and whatever his private opinion might have been the bos'n was too good a disciplinarian to show anything in front of one of the boys.

After supper Mr Howarth, Mr Rees, Robin and Timothy Ballard started to overhaul the engine. They got the valve cover off, dismantled the timing gear and lifted the cylinder head. The cause of the failure was at once obvious. The cylinders were full of water which had flooded in from a badly perished rubber seal on the cooling water system between the block and the head. It was one thing drying the plugs and the cylinders, but when they found that water had seeped past the piston rings contaminating the oil in the sump, Robin thought the end had come. Both boys were dead tired.

The thought of having to take off the sump covers to bail the warm, heavy black oil out with cigarette tins, nauseated them. But they put a good face on it and set to work while Neil Townrow was sent off to brew a mug of cocoa.

As the boys worked, Howarth and Rees improvised a new ring from part of the inner tube of a car wheel. The job was going fairly well when there was the sound of an angry voice up on deck. It turned out to be the Captain who was peering into the compass bowl now lit by the small oil-lamp.

'Mr Howarth!' he bellowed. 'Be good enough to look at this.'

The bos'n made his way up as fast as his vast frame and the narrow ladder would allow.

'Yes, sir, what's wrong?'

'Wrong, man! Look at the compass card. It's floating in milk.'

Howarth peered at it. Sure enough, it seemed to be floating in some strange, white liquid. He turned to the Captain:

'Can't understand it, sir. Naylor and I topped it up with the spirit he bought ashore earlier on. We got the bubble out and she seemed fine.'

'Send for Naylor and fetch the spirit.'

Captain Drew had had about enough for one day. Whatever the cause, the instrument would now have to be drained and refilled before they could get away tomorrow.

Squeak arrived with the bottle. The skipper took one look and all but threw the two of them over the side.

'You idiot!' he thundered. 'Can't you see that this is a surgical spirit? When you mix it with the stuff in the compass, the water in it causes the whole thing to become opaque. Get started and unship the thing, drain it and have it ready for refilling tomorrow morning.' Still fuming, he stamped off below to his cabin, leaving everyone including the bos'n looking most uncomfortable.

By nine next morning things looked better again. The engine had been reassembled and, for the time being at least, was clanking away. The compass was in the process of being rinsed out before being recharged with fresh spirit which the ship chandler had brought aboard at very short notice. By eleven o'clock *Venturer* was clear of the last lock, ready to head up the first stage of the Canal through Loch Dochfour to Loch Ness.

Although hard worked, the boys realised that a ship's complement has to shake down. They knew that the first day or two would be hard going but it didn't worry them. Most of them had been up to Inverness by sea at some time, so the experience was not altogether new.

But the Canal was something quite different. Jackie Main was the only one who had been through before, in his father's fishing boat. He and Percy Chester emerged as the authorities on the Canal. Percy gained his knowledge from the charts in which he had suddenly taken a keen interest—some said to avoid the unpleasant jobs around the ship. Be that as it may, he knew quite a lot about it. Even Captain Drew respected his knowledge.

They were approaching the swing bridge by Tomnahurich, where the Inverness–Fort Augustus road crosses the Canal. The boys found it thrilling to see the bridge open in answer to the foghorn's blast, while cars queued up on either side and passengers came out to wish them good luck. Just as they were abeam of the bridge Robin spun round to the Captain.

'There it is, sir,' he said. 'I am certain it is the same car.'

'What car, lad?' Drew looked up the road in the direction of Robin's outstretched arm.

'The same one that I saw down by the sea lock when we came in. The black one with the three men in it. I'm not quite certain, but I believe that it was an Alvis.'

'I see, I see. So we are to be trailed all the way down the Canal. They searched and failed in Inverness. I wonder what will be the next move?' Drew's mouth, as he spoke, was drawn into a thin, hard line, while his eyes had a peculiarly deceptive lazy look, which some who knew him better had come to recognise as a sign of imminent action.

Up for'ard the boys were discussing the Canal and its peculiarities.

'Hey, Chester,' someone shouted. 'How long is this waterway?'

'Sixty miles from sea to sea.'

'What is the deepest point?'

'Something like one hundred and twenty-nine

fathoms in the vicinity of Castle Urquhart on Loch Ness. They say that is where the monster is most often seen. Pretty deep if you ask me,' Percy went on, munching an apple.

'How many lochs do we pass through?'

Percy thought for a moment. 'Three, if you don't count Loch Dochfour—it's the small one just short of Loch Ness. It has a long weir where the river flows away from the Canal. We have to go through the flood lock at Dochgarroch before we enter it. After Loch Ness there is Loch Oich and then Loch Lochy.

'You seem to know all the answers,' Neil Townrow piped up. 'How high do we go in the course of the passage?'

Percy was ready for this one.

'Well,' he began, 'there are twenty locks in all. Loch Oich is about a hundred feet above the high-water mark at the Beauly end where the average rise and fall is thirteen feet six inches for spring tides, but only six feet three inches for neaps.'

'Well, you swot!' exclaimed Naylor. 'Any more words of wisdom, Master Mariner?'

Percy looked round to be sure of his audience. 'Well, I can give you the positions of the locks if you like,' he said trying to appear offhand.

'Go on. Bet you can't.'

'Right then, here we go. Two at Clachnaharry, four at Muirtown, one at Dochgarroch, five at Fort Augustus, one at Kytra, one at Cullochy, two at Laggan, two at Gairlochy, eight at Benavie and three at Corpach. There—see!'

Percy sat looking suitably smug, as he added: 'And any vessel can use the Canal up to a hundred and sixty feet in length, thirty-five feet beam and with a draught of not more than nine feet. For further information see Admiralty Chart Number 1791.' So saying he threw the core of his apple overboard and nipped down to the saloon.

'He's a pompous devil but he knows his stuff,' laughed Timothy. 'Wish I knew it half as well. Hey, what's that?' he said, suddenly pointing ahead as the ship rounded a bend.

'Why, that's Torveau,' replied Robin, 'and those are the pylons carrying the power lines over the Canal which limit mast height to a hundred and twenty feet above water level, I think.'

'But what is that below the wires?' Timothy went on. 'Don't you see it? Looks like a rope to me. I'm going for the glasses.' He raced along aft.

Two seconds later he called anxiously: 'Robin, it is a rope. There are men on both pylons as well. Better get the skipper.'

But Captain Drew had already heard the conversation and was on deck. He sized up the situation in an instant.

'Mr Howarth,' he called down the after hatch, 'stop both engines, quick. Trenchard, go for'ard. Be prepared for anything, but don't move till I give the order. It will take us all our time to stop her. Take all the boys clear of the mast with you.'

There was the sound of hammering from below.

'Mr Howarth, stop both engines immediately. This is an emergency.' Clearly the skipper was getting angry. 'Quick man, we have no time to lose.'

Venturer was approaching the rope fast. As things stood it would catch her just below the topmast.

'What are they doing there anyway? There was no word of this from the Canal office.' Still muttering, he dashed back to the hatch.

'Stop both!' he yelled.

The rope was now only two hundred yards away. Howarth's head came out of the depths to meet him, his face purple.

'Sir,' he gasped, 'the port engine has jammed in gear. I can't free the clutch.'

As he spoke the starboard one coughed, spluttered twice and then became silent.

Venturer moved on towards the rope.

Chapter VII

TROUBLE IN THE CANAL

As the engine spluttered to a stop Howarth leapt from the companion-way to the engine-room, trying in desperation to disengage the jammed clutch lever. With one motor dead, he dare not cut the other while there was time or the faintest chance of getting things freed. One look at the skipper's face had been enough to convince him of the gravity of the situation and he had only seconds in which to act.

Captain Drew, however, was not taking any chances. ' Clear the chain locker and stand by to let go the port anchor ! ' he called out.

Robin had seen this coming. As soon as he had gone for'ard, he had sent two hands to lift the galley deck which covered the anchor cable so leaving the chain free to run.

' Chain locker clear, sir,' he reported. ' Port anchor ready for lowering.'

' Let go port anchor ! '

' Let go port anchor,' came the echo.

With a quick look round to see that no-one was in danger, and a hurried check that the windlass was free, Robin hit the pin on the ' cat's head '. The quick release gear freed the anchor from the massive bracket which held it suspended over the side. It struck the water with a tremendous splash, boring down to the bottom of the Canal and dragging the cable from the locker up over the windlass in a crescendo of noise. The boys for'ard were stunned by the din and blinded by the dust.

'Check her!' The order thundered from aft.

'Check her, sir!' Robin shouted back as he applied the brake to the rattling chain.

'Ship on the port bow heading straight for us!' came a cry from the look-out.

Drew was at the rail in an instant, looking to where the boy was excitedly pointing. He saw it at once, the long, low, grey hull of a motor torpedo boat bearing down on them. Almost as soon as the look-out called, the boys had heard the voice of its powerful engines when it rounded the bend ahead.

'Haul away on that line, Mr Rees,' Drew ordered.

'Aye, aye, sir,' the Welshman replied as he heaved on the rope, bending his back to put all his weight into it.

When the port anchor had rattled away for'ard, Rees had toppled the smaller kedge anchor over the stern, but had put no strain on it until Howarth in desperation switched off the other engine with the clutch still jammed.

As the weight of the ship came on the for'ard cable the stern started to swing to starboard towards the bank. It was this swing that Rees was now trying to check. Leaving the stern rope taut and taking a turn round the bits when he could, he knew that unless he succeeded, *Venturer* would be lying athwart the Canal, blocking the fairway.

What happened next no-one ever quite knew for certain. As the M.T.B. hove in sight the rope which had been suspended between the pylons was cast off by someone on shore. It flew through the sheaves with a rush to splash into the water not six feet in front of the ship's bowsprit.

Rushing to look over the side the boys were just able to make out the shape of the manilla line as it sank slowly into the depths.

At the same time pandemonium seemed to break out in the heaving scrub on the Canal bank. The men on the pylons had vanished, but from the undergrowth came the sounds of shouting as people dashed wildly away from the water in the direction of a rough track leading towards the main road.

On top of everything else came the roar of the naval ship's engines going full astern to avoid getting her screws fouled by the rope. When her stern approached the bank a number of sailors jumped ashore in pursuit of the men who had fled. They struggled through the waist-high bracken as best they could, but long before they scaled the steep scarp the sound of a car engine drawing away rapidly in bottom gear told that the others had escaped.

The M.T.B. had made fast to a couple of trees ashore, while her Captain, a young Lieutenant, came to have a word with Captain Drew.

'Any idea what's going on, sir?' he asked after he got aboard. 'That had the makings of a first-class pile-up.'

'I thought they were men from the hydro board working on the overhead cables,' Drew replied, 'but the Canal office gave us no warning of them. And anyway,' he continued rather thoughtfully, 'they would hardly have run away as soon as you showed up if they had been honest workmen.'

At that moment a petty officer approached, saluted smartly and reported that the shore party had recovered the rope, blocks and other equipment which had been used. After some further discussions it was decided that the M.T.B. should take the tackle to Inverness, there to make a full report to the police and Canal authorities.

Captain Drew took his leave of the Lieutenant and in doing so asked him to send the youngsters aboard from his own vessel where they had gone as though attracted by a magnet. In fact, had he only known it, at that very moment Percy was enjoying some fruit salad in the M.T.B.'s galley !

In the meantime, while the skippers had been talking, Howarth and Rees had succeeded in freeing the jammed clutch with the help of the naval engineers. They had also begged some material from which to cut new rings for the other engine.

With everyone aboard, Drew blew ' stand-by '. The crew fell in at ' harbour stations ', and when all was ready he gave the order to ' slack away for'ard, haul taut aft.' When the stern was over the kedge anchor in midstream, they hauled it aboard.

' Start heaving away for'ard.'

The boys manned the windlass handles, singing as they started the tedious job of winding in the heavy cable. As she took the strain, the bow swung away from the bank out into midstream.

Drew had been coaxing her ahead on the one engine, taking up the slack. Now, as the report came ' Anchor up ! ' he gave the order, ' Slow ahead.'

' Slow ahead,' came the engineer's reply, and while *Venturer* gathered speed they turned to wave to the M.T.B. casting off her ropes in preparation for her run down to Inverness.

The post mortem on the morning's events between the Captain, Howarth and Rees had been interrupted as they manoeuvred the ship through the flood lock at Dochgarroch. Then, safely past the narrows at Bara Light, the ship nosed out into the centre of Loch Ness.

Rees was busy showing the boys how to stream the log while Howarth was below working on the 'dead' engine. The Captain was not sorry that the conversation had had to be broken off. He had found it difficult to work up much enthusiasm for the views of the bos'n and his mate as they fumed about the criminal negligence of the authorities. Well he knew that the rope had nothing to do with electrical repairs.

As he had said to Robin during a couple of minutes' brief rest and chat, no-one would be more surprised than the hydro board when they heard about the affair. What would have happened if the M.T.B. had not come in sight, was something that Drew did not care to think about. Certainly its timely arrival had foiled that plan. But now . . .

The schooner forged ahead as best she could with her one screw over the waters of the loch. Abeam of Tor Point, the galley hands announced that grub was ready and it was agreed that as it was such a glorious day, all hands should eat on deck. Due to the interruptions of the morning the meal was light—or was supposed to be. The menu read: Noodle soup (from packets), Salad and Potatoes. This was followed by Squeak Naylor's special effort, Canadian crusty pie. All went well till the last course when things got stuck good and fast, literally.

It looked appetising enough on the plate, a sort of crumbly pastry with stewed fruit. To see it, no-one could have guessed that it had the consistency of bird lime. It was the poor old bos'n who went aground first. He took a hefty mouthful but forgot that, though the other two items were cool enough, the custard was piping hot. While the yellow liquid seared his tongue, he made frantic efforts to open his mouth but alas, in vain.

The sticky pastry had securely fastened both sets of teeth together and try as he might he could accomplish nothing but a series of muffled grunts. With a handkerchief over his mouth he danced a weird hornpipe around the after deck, and though everyone roared with laughter, Mr Howarth found it anything but funny. Both his mouth and his dignity had suffered.

No-one had much success with the pudding. One gull got into difficulties similar to those of the bos'n when it greedily snatched up a piece which someone had thrown overboard, only to find its beak well and truly gummed up. It was last seen bobbing about on the wake astern, angrily shaking its head from side to side as it plunged its beak beneath the water in the hope of ridding itself of the cloying mass.

Though Squeak strenuously denied that he had bungled the recipe, something had obviously gone wrong. It was left to Robin to solve the mystery. The book had recommended so many ounces of flour, and this the budding chef had added. What he didn't know was that the divisions on the antiquated scales represented 'pounds'. No wonder that instead of having enough pastry to cover two large pie dishes he had sufficient to carpet the ship above and below decks as well.

That night they lay up at the top of the locks by Fort Augustus. On thinking things over, Drew was of the opinion that his enemies would not try any more frontal attacks—not for the moment at any rate. Still, he saw the local police, explaining that his room had been broken into in Inverness and asked them to give him a guard. Though they obviously thought him something of a fuss-pot, they did what he asked and stationed a man on board during the hours of darkness.

The following day, after a morning dip in the clear waters of the Canal, the boys set about washing down the decks in preparation for an early start. It was a beautiful sail through the river Oich and on down the loch of the same name to the swing bridge at Laggan, with its two locks nestling in the shade of Ben Tigh, known locally as Glengarry's Bowling Green.

Both engines were functioning once more, but obviously in poor shape. The Captain had discussed the matter with Mr Howarth and Mr Rees. Though reluctant to put off any time at all, they could not risk the trip down the west coast of Scotland with unreliable engines. Besides, they would have to be able to call on full power when they passed through the Menai Straits. There was nothing for it but to put in at Oban where the shore-side engineers could overhaul the defective seals.

Secretly everyone was quite pleased at the prospect of spending a few days in a new port—all that is, except Robin and the Captain, for whom time in port meant just so many hours during which their enemy might strike again.

While *Venturer* sailed on down Loch Lochy, the two talked it over, trying to foresee every possible way in which an attack might develop, hoping by this means to prevent the plans going astray.

The trip to Corpach proved uneventful, as Captain Drew had foreseen. They worked the ship down through the eight locks at Benavie and the three remaining ones at Corpach itself. Before leaving this village at the western end of the Canal, the skipper phoned Inverness to see if there was any news of those responsible for the rope incident. There was, however, nothing fresh. Neither the Canal authorities nor the hydro board knew anything about it, and the police had so far failed to find any clue to the identity of the men. Drew was not surprised.

Venturer turned south and then west, pushing her long bowsprit ahead of her down Loch Eil towards the open sea. To port could be seen the huge mass of Ben Nevis reaching skywards behind Fort William. By the rail, Robin and Tony looked longingly at the mountain as they recalled the various week-ends which they had spent climbing there during expeditions from School.

While the towering rocks fell away astern the helmsman steadied the schooner on course for the passage through the narrows at Corran Ferry. Once clear of the lighthouse on the point, the wind freshened a little, whipping a fine spray inboard over the port quarter.

After the even passage of the inland waterway, it was good to feel the deck heave as *Venturer* heeled over under her foresail, mainsail, staysail, inner and outer jibs. Her course lay down Loch Linnhe, past the island of Lismore to Oban.

Captain Drew had shut off the engines just as soon as they had made sail in Loch Linnhe, partly to conserve what life was left in them, partly because he hated the things, but accepted them as a necessary evil.

As they crossed the head of the Firth of Lorne, the breeze freshened to about force four or four and a half. The old ship seemed to sense her approaching meeting with the Atlantic. The wind thrummed in the rigging. With each fresh gust the lee scuppers went under, allowing the cold green sea to gush up through the wash ports and slosh about the wooden deck.

Suddenly there came a shout from aft, by the binnacle. Mr Howarth had noticed that a tarpaulin on the lifeboat had worked slack and was in danger of blowing overboard.

But though he bellowed hard, his voice was drowned by the noise of the elements. Unable to stand it any longer he strode boldly up the slippery deck, shouting to the group of boys gathered by the lee of the for'ard companion-way as he went.

But this was not Mr Howarth's day. His teeth, already the cause of certain hilarity, came unshipped under the strain of his efforts. They flew between the boat and the rail with a clatter, being saved from a watery grave only by the quick reaction of Jackie Main, who dived down to snatch them back as they slid towards the open scupper.

Their near loss was grief enough to the bos'n, but the roars of laughter with which the accident was received struck a mortal blow to his dignity once again. Any idea of retaliation, however, was banished as the whistle blew for stand-by.

Venturer had been weaving her way through a convoy engaged in forming up, in preparation for an Atlantic crossing, they supposed.

Painted battleship grey, the ships sat low in the water, vessels of every size and type laden to their 'North Atlantic' marks. One or two flew barrage balloons designed to prevent aircraft making low-level attacks on them. The whole scene struck a sombre note which served to remind the crew of the schooner that this was indeed war and that after the comparatively pleasant run through the Canal they had to face the dangerous sail from Oban to Aberdovey.

'Signal station calling up, sir.'

'Answer it,' Drew replied.

Robin picked up the Aldis lamp and gave a long flash. Back came the winking light: BT—the break sign, followed by the message: 'What ship?'

The Captain had read the signal as it came in.

'Tell them, Trenchard,' he said.

Robin gave a succession of A's, received an answering flash, passed the break sign and followed up with the ship's name.

Back came the instruction: 'Anchor your vessel in berth T4.'

'Good,' exclaimed the Captain. 'Couldn't be better. Down mainsail, Mr Howarth.'

CHAPTER VIII

AN ADDITION TO THE CREW

'DOWN foresail.'

'Down foresail, sir.'

The boys smartly cast off throat, peak and topping-lift halyards, hauling the boom inboard with the sheets as the skipper swung the ship up into the wind.

'Back headsails to windward.'

Eager hands goose-winged the two jibs and staysail, so taking the way off her while she came up to her anchorage. Slowly the schooner came to rest, paused and then started to drop astern.

'Let go port anchor.'

'Let go, sir.'

There was a rumble as the chain whipped up over the windlass and out through the hawser hole.

'Check her.'

'Check, sir.' Robin swiftly screwed up the brake on the drum. The anchor bit into the bottom of the bay.

'Slack away.'

'Slack away, sir.'

'What depth of water are we in, Chester?' Drew asked.

Percy checked the bearings on the chart. 'Ten fathoms, sir,' he sang out.

'How much cable will you want then?'

'About thirty, sir,' came the reply.

'Good. We are fairly well protected here—give

her twenty-six and let me know when it is on the windlass.'

'Aye, aye, sir.'

Robin eased the wheel, watching the painted marks on the cable as each shackle went outboard. When the required amount of cable lay on the bottom, he screwed up the windlass and reported to the Captain.

'That will do. Down head sails, on stoppers and lower away the dinghy.' The Captain turned as he spoke to check the anchor bearings.

The anchorage was pretty crowded, and in bringing his ship to rest dead on the spot given to him by Naval Control, Drew had now shown himself for the fine seaman that he was.

He despised engines, and delighted in handling his ship without their clanging, smelly aid. But though the exercise had been fun it had also been a lesson in seamanship to his crew. Its successful completion had set the seal on their admiration for him.

As soon as the vessel was squared up, the Captain ordered the boat's party to bring the dinghy round to the pilot ladder, now hanging over the quarter. Taking his brief-case containing the ship's papers he set off for Naval Control to report and obtain further clearance. But before going he left orders that no-one was to come on board without his special permission.

Timothy was in charge of the boat's party. Knowing that everyone would be idly watching the performance of the men, he saw to it that the rowing was perfect.

'In—out ; in—out ; in—out,' he gave them a

short, quick stroke in the choppy waters of the harbour. The small boat sped over the distance to the quayside and in no time, as it seemed, they were making fast to the stone steps alongside a dozen other similar craft.

'I shall be back in an hour,' the Captain said. 'During that time, I want one man on board, but you can take it in turns if you like.' So saying, he climbed the slippery green steps to vanish amid the throng above.

An hour later to the minute, they were ready to cast off again when a man pushed his way to the head of the steps and hailed them.

'Ahoy there!'

The Captain looked up. 'Yes?' he called back.

'Are you the *Venturer*'s boat?'

'Yes.'

'Can you take me out to her?' By this time he was half-way down the steps.

'I am Captain Drew.' The skipper stood up in the stern sheets, holding out his hand. Carefully, the other made his way down the remainder of the treacherous flight.

'How do you do, sir. My name is McCann. I am an engineer from Glasgow. The Company sent me to join you for the remainder of the voyage to Aberdovey. The Marine Superintendent said that you were having engine trouble of a rather serious nature, and I was ordered to report here as soon as possible.'

'Yes, yes, I know about you,' Drew replied. 'Come aboard. The office said they would try to spare someone, though I hardly expected to see you so soon.'

McCann climbed into the stern sheets.

'Take her away, Ballard,' the skipper called out.

Timothy gripped the short tiller. This was what he enjoyed. All the boys liked boat handling; it created a healthy rivalry among them since each strived to put on the best show.

'Toss oars; let go for'ard.'

The bow painter splashed into the water as it was hauled inboard.

'Down port oars; back water port.'

Slowly the stem swung away from the quay.

'Fend off with the loom of the oar, starboard bow.'

The bow-man bore against the stone, pushing the fore end out into the harbour.

'Down starboard oars when you're clear.'

As the blades struck the water, Timothy deftly slipped the stern rope from the metal ring ashore. 'Oars!' he shouted.

Port gave one more stroke and came to rest, blades flat, a foot above the water, 'Give way!' Bodies leant well aft towards the stern. 'Together!'

The wood bit deep into the oily water as the first three short strokes put way on her, sending the little craft darting out towards the open water.

'Well done, youngster.' The remark came from a Chief Petty Officer standing at the rail of a naval launch. Timothy felt a glow spreading over his face. Drew laughed.

'You won't often get a compliment like that,' he said. 'Nice work.'

Timothy felt very pleased. It didn't often turn out just as smoothly. Something usually went wrong, leaving you looking foolish. With a shock he suddenly remembered. . . .

' In fenders ! ' he ordered.

On board again everyone was in the saloon. Drew took McCann below to meet Mr Howarth and Mr Rees while Timothy sought out Robin, who was for'ard doing a bit of splicing.

' What's he like,' Robin asked, ' this engineer ? '

Timothy paused before replying. ' Hard to say,' he said at length. ' Small, dark with black, beady eyes. He sports a thin moustache and walks with a slight stoop, like most engineers on ships. His accent is odd ; at first it appears to be Scottish, but I can't place it at all. He seems to alter it at times. Otherwise, he is much what you would expect.'

In his cabin, Captain Drew read the note from Glasgow which McCann had given him. It was on Company notepaper, but the signature was illegible. However, it bore the rubber stamp of the ' Marine Super's Office '. It told Drew that McCann had been torpedoed off Freetown while in his previous ship. He was one of the few survivors and had been pretty badly shocked, so much so in fact, that even now he wouldn't talk about it or about any of his other trips. He was a good engineer, apparently, and had wide experience of petrol-paraffin engines.

That explained a lot, Drew thought, as he filed the letter away. He had wondered why McCann had seemed reticent about his other jobs with the Company. Anyway, he was here now, and could get cracking right away on the machines. That was the main thing.

By the following afternoon the engineer had stripped both engines down and had pronounced them to be in a dreadful state. Repairs, he said, would take considerably longer than had first been anticipated, and he bitterly blamed the people in Darroch for letting *Venturer* sail with her auxiliaries in such poor shape.

His estimation proved to be fairly accurate. Spares were hard to get, and by the time she was ready for sea again, twelve days had slipped past.

The crew had enjoyed the stay. The boys turned to at seven in the morning and finished at four in the afternoon. From then on they were free to go ashore to the pictures, sail the small dinghy or, as many often did, to wander aboard other ships in the harbour to drink cocoa and listen to the tales of men who had been at sea all their lives.

Drew very soon saw that security in and around Oban was strict. Not only was it a busy convoy centre with numerous ships, both merchant and naval, arriving and departing, but close by, on the island of Kerrera, there was a large flying-boat base for the Catalinas.

Indeed, it was from here that such a plane on patrol was to shadow the *Bismarck* in one of the epic actions of the war at sea.

With naval launches moving about the anchorage day and night, no-one was likely to interfere with them, Drew thought. Neither he nor Robin went ashore more than was absolutely essential. On the few occasions on which they had landed, they had gone together, without rousing any suspicion.

At last everything seemed ready for the next step. They had taken on extra water and more stores, particularly fresh meat to replace that which had gone bad and had to be dumped a couple of days after leaving Darroch. At the time when Drew discovered that the butcher had let them down, he would have murdered that worthy had he been able to lay hands on him.

From the Firth of Lorne their course lay south through the Sounds of Luing and Jura and thence to the Mull of Kintyre. The day on which they left Oban saw a light breeze blowing from the south-west.

Once again Drew showed his capabilities as a seaman by weighing anchor without the aid of the engines, but though the wind was favourable for this particular operation it was less to their liking as it headed them when they turned south, necessitating long tacks down the Firth.

As the schooner left the bay a car started up on the road above the town. It was an Alvis, the same one which Robin had seen at Inverness, the same one which watched *Venturer* from the little town of Onich as she entered Loch Linnhe ; the same one which sped on to Oban via the Ballachulish Ferry and Connel Bridge.

Now, with its sinister occupants, it roared south once more on the road to Kilninver, Clachan Bridge and Seil. Once over the bridge it followed a tortuous route through Balvicar towards a point on the rocky coast known as Dun Mucaig, a ruined stronghold standing on high ground with a bay beneath.

When the road stopped, the men in the car got out. Without a word they lifted their haversacks and struck northwards. Presently they waited.

Far out in the Firth, *Venturer* went about, heading once more towards Argyll. The wind, which had freshened for an hour or so, now died away leaving behind a heavy swell. Everyone on board had found his sea legs except McCann. It was his first time in a sailing ship and he was having a gruelling baptism.

As they approached the coast, Drew looked worried. 'We don't have enough way on to put her about, Mr Howarth,' he said. 'Better tell McCann to start up the port engine—the one motor should be enough to push her round.'

'Very good, sir,' the bos'n replied, setting off to find the engineer.

At last he ran him to earth between the rail and the lifeboat, for'ard. He was peering away out over the waters towards the heavy, lowering cliffs of the foreshore, looking anything but happy.

'Skipper says as wot you 'ad better ginger up your port motor, mate.' With his message the bos'n gave McCann a hearty whack on the back which all but put him over the ship's side.

The engineer gripped his stomach as he rolled his eyes heavenwards.

'Easy, bos'n, easy. We're not all men who have served before the mast.' Another spasm caught him, preventing further speech.

''Ere, you're proper done up—you'd better turn in while I get that scrap heap ticking. Off you go below.'

'No, no. I'm all right, Mr Howarth, really I am. It will pass. It's going now.' Clutching the rail he kept staring out over the sea to where the swell flung itself in fury against the jagged rocks.

'Bos'n, what's happened to that engine? If we don't get the thing started we'll be aground.'

'Aye, that's it—aground,' McCann whispered with a twisted smile.

Howarth rounded on him: 'Wot you say, Mr McCann?'

'Me? Nothing. I mentioned that I'd better be getting around, that's all.' And he vanished below.

'Mr Howarth, have you told . . .?'

'Yes, sir. The engineer 'as gone below now. Should have the motor going in a couple of ticks.'

'If he doesn't, things will be darned difficult,' said Drew grimly.

Away to windward the skipper saw the darkening water beneath a heavy squall. It looked extensive and quite fierce, though it approached slowly. He went to the hatch and called:

'What's wrong below?'

'Have her going any moment now, sir,' came the reply.

'Then hurry up, will you.'

Dead ahead they could see the line of surf; could hear its hollow pounding echoing from the many caves around. Suddenly Drew called out: 'Trenchard!'

'Yes, sir.'

'Clear away port anchor.'

'Very good, sir.'

Robin ran for'ard to execute the order when the engine broke into life.

'Thank goodness!' exclaimed the skipper. 'Stand by to go about. Lee helm, quartermaster. Let fly fore sheets; aft main sheets. Full ahead, Mr McCann.'

Venturer was dangerously close inshore now, almost beneath the high cliffs. Slowly her head came round under the power of the port screw. It seemed to take hours for her to make up into the wind but at last she made it, hanging there rolling heavily, her sails flapping from side to side.

Then it happened. The noise of the engine faltered, picked up, faltered again and stopped. Quick as a flash Drew shouted :

'Let go port anchor ! ' But his blood froze when Robin yelled back :

'Can't, sir. Windlass has jammed in gear.'

There was only one chance left. Robin and the bos'n knew what that was, and they had already acted without waiting for further orders. Each seized a corner of a head sail and leaning far out, dangerously far out over the ship's side, was backing it to windward in the hope of driving the bow round on to the new tack.

Aft, by the steering box, Mr Rees feverishly tried to clear the small kedge anchor. It might hold her, but it was a forlorn hope. And so she stuck there, drifting towards the hungry rocks in a moment of suspense which was to stamp itself on the mind of every man on board.

Abaft the beam, in an inlet some four hundred yards away, the telegraph tinkled in the engine-room of a long, black power boat. With the summons : 'Full ahead two', the low, thin hull shook as the craft leapt ahead to throw herself at the narrow entrance protecting her from the open sea.

She had some twenty yards to go between narrow walls of rock and had all but won clear when a gigantic wave lifted the plywood bow out of the water to dash it to pieces on the rock and weed of the shore on the port hand side. The helmsman never had a chance, for the launch's power was her own undoing. Once off the narrow channel she drove herself to destruction.

Glancing aft, Drew was in time to see the crash, but it was not till long after that he was able to piece the bits together. For, as the launch struck the rocks, the squall hit the schooner. The staysail was torn from the bos'n's grasp, leaving Robin as the only means of ensuring that the vessel made the new tack.

Arms aching, he clung on grimly while the wind tore at the canvas. Little by little she fell away to starboard. He heard from somewhere far away, as in a dream, the Captain's voice calling: 'Let draw!'

With her crew sweating to haul aft the sheets, *Venturer*'s sails filled with a rush. They were scarcely able to take a turn on the cleats before the deck canted at a crazy angle, while the foam churned out from under her stern not thirty yards from the rocks.

Searching the coast with his glasses, Drew could see no sign of the power boat save some small pieces of driftwood. She had sunk without a trace and from that cauldron nothing would ever be recovered.

On the cliff path above, a lone watcher shrugged his shoulders, put on his pack and started the long walk back to the Alvis.

Chapter IX

VENTURER SPRINGS A LEAK

It had been a terribly near thing and everyone on board knew it. The ship had all but foundered on the dangerous rocks, and but for the courageous way in which Robin Trenchard had clung to the sheet, forcing the jib out to windward, *Venturer* would have been dashed to pieces on the coast of Scotland.

As he made his way below Drew felt quite sick with the thought of what might have happened. He went slowly into his cabin to sit down for a moment before going on to see McCann in the engine-room.

Had he really left it too late before going about? If the engineer had got the motor going as soon as the order had been given there would have been plenty of time. Still, it had taken him longer than the skipper had expected, so that was that.

Had he acted correctly when once it had been started up? Drew cast his mind back. Yes, he thought that he had acted in a seamanlike manner. He had given it a minute or two to settle, and had then put her about. If the screw had not stopped at that very moment she would have been round safely. It was a coincidence, he reflected, that the engineer should be the man associated with both the first and second set of circumstances. And then there was the black launch. No-one else had apparently seen the incident. At least he had not heard any of the crew mention it. Recalling the sight of the craft striking the rocks made him shudder. What their plan might have been he could not guess, but he was certain that those manning the power boat were no friends of his.

While sitting thinking, Drew had been idly flicking over the papers on his desk. Suddenly he whipped his pipe from his mouth, a puzzled frown on his face. Yes ! He was certain of it. Someone had again searched his room. With the realization that they were now out into the open sea, bound by radio silence and with an enemy on board, the Captain felt the hair on the back of his neck rise.

In the engine-room a figure sat by the silent machine brooding over the chance that was gone. Drew had been wrong when he supposed that no-one else had seen the black launch vanish. McCann had seen it go, and in his black heart he cursed the men that had died with her for a set of incompetent idiots. Fools that they were to have bungled a simple plan so carefully laid. But for their stupidity the launch could have been on its way to Ireland by now, to where a plane waited ready to take the secrets of the new camera to those who would pay most.

And the *Venturer*, with the lives of those aboard her ? McCann's thin lips curled in a sneer. Why should a man prepared to sell his country worry about a few boys with a wooden ship who were playing at being sailors ? With a bang of his fist upon the valve cover, he dismissed them from his mind. The babies, he thought, they should have stayed with their mothers ; stuck to their trains and other toys, and left the work of war to men who were used to its ruthless demands.

The engineer was furious, thwarted and in an ugly temper. He had worked the details out so well, had tried to make allowances for everything, but how, he asked himself, could he have foreseen that the numbskulls given to him for accomplices would ram the rocks first shot, kill themselves and wreck the launch which it had taken him a week to procure ?

In his disappointment he strode like a caged beast around the tiny engine-room, while with every step his temper rose as he thought of their respective roles in this drama. It was he, McCann, who had to do all the thinking, lay all the schemes, take all the chances. The other boobs had to bring the launch out and lay her alongside, but even this had proved to be beyond their feeble capabilities. Still, they had paid the price of their incompetence. But he—he alone could acquire the vital package, the sheaf of blueprints on which so much depended. And when once he had them well away from the cursed ship he would see to it that only he would reap the reward of his plotting.

In a moment his self-assurance left him. He sank like a jaded toy balloon on the tool-box beside the engines.

'When once he had them !' But he *didn't* have them. He had thought that all he had to do was to go to the Captain's desk and the plans would be there. He clutched the cold exhaust manifold to steady himself as the schooner lurched in the rising sea. He wasn't over-worried. They were in the cabin somewhere ; of that he felt confident.

Though his cursory search had failed to reveal them, he knew that when the time came for him to rip the place apart they would be there. Oh yes, they would be there all right. Nothing would stop him from seizing them and then——

Footsteps approached from aft. 'You there, Mr McCann?' It was the skipper's voice.

In an instant the fury and venom were wiped from his face to be replaced by a look of servility. Quickly he began uncoupling the carburettor as Drew's figure filled the doorway.

'What went wrong with your engines—eh?'

Up on deck the duty watch sheltered behind the boats as the keen, cold spray lashed the superstructure about them. The weather, unpredictable as ever, had changed to a strong, steady blow from the south. The wind was increasing, giving promise of a dirty night. Heavy rain clouds hung low on the horizon, the barometer was falling and Squeak Naylor had picked up a most unpromising weather forecast on the ship's set. *Venturer* was bathed in a greenish light.

'Don't mind admitting I was a bit scared earlier on,' Chester said.

'Was rather a near thing,' Ballard agreed, 'but the old man knows what he's doing. He's a terrific seaman, you know.'

'This bit of the coast gives me the willies. What between being nearly sunk on the rocks one minute and having to settle down for a night of wind for another, give me a farm! Anyway, this light's eerie. Everyone looks as if they are about to be sick.' Clearly Jackie Main was getting fed up.

'Joking apart, you fellows, there is something

fishy about this ship.' For a few seconds there was silence among the boys. Chester had said in words what most of them had privately felt. Timothy thought that as the senior present he must take the lead.

'Oh, come, Percy, that fertile imagination of yours has run riot again. Fishy? With Captain Drew, Mr Rees and Mr Howarth aboard? Don't be dim.'

'All right, Ballard, I'm dim am I?' retorted Chester, now thoroughly roused. 'Then how do you explain the behaviour of your precious pal, Trenchard, for a start, let alone the various things that keep going wrong every little while?'

Timothy winced. He had noticed the change in his friend. Usually full of fun, always ready with a quick retort, he was now pale-looking with a white, drawn face. Several people had noticed him often standing alone leaning over the ship's rail gazing out to sea, and had put it down to his feeling seasick or to being a little off colour. Chester's forthright remarks had exposed things in a rather different light. But this feeling had to be squashed. It was bad for morale—this Timothy instinctively understood. Had he been present Robin would have jumped on it, he felt sure.

'This has gone far enough now,' he said, standing up and looking the others up and down with all the authority of his position. 'Granted, some things do call for an explanation, and that Robin has not been himself of late, but that does not mean to say that there is anything "fishy" as you put it. I tell you what—I'll have a word with Robin as soon as possible, to try and find out whether there is any real significance behind the events to which you refer. We must not start a scare, at all costs.'

The others had little option but to agree, because just as Timothy finished speaking, *Venturer* threw herself high in the air as she met an enormous wave. At the apex of her climb the vessel executed a half roll before beginning the downward plunge again. The deck now being wet and slippery the boys had their work cut out to remain upright. With arms flaying wildly they clutched at anything which afforded means of support.

Percy grabbed a nearby line only to find, too late, that it was not secured at either end. He disappeared feet first into the scuppers in a welter of oilskins, sea boots and old rope. His training for rugger tackles stood him in good stead. Having been taught how to fall without hurting himself, he escaped with nothing worse than a few bruises.

As the schooner steadied herself, there came a call from below. ' Duty hands to starboard for'ard store. She's making water—quick ! '

At the summons the boys tumbled down the hatch to find Mr Howarth battling with a leaking plug in the ship's side. The trouble came from the space where the outlet pipe from a pump had once passed outboard. When it had been removed, the hole had been stopped with a wooden peg. Owing to the incessant pounding, this had worked slack with the result that a fair amount of water was sloshing around the deck of the place, soaking the various sacks.

First job was to remove the gear. After that the bos'n secured the bung with a heavy mallet. The watch then went to work bailing the water, and finally everything was put back and squared off to prevent its moving with the motion of the ship.

Darkness found the *Venturer* tacking backwards and forwards, fighting hard for every cable made good over the ground. Her course lay through the Sound of Jura, and to pass safely, Drew knew that he would need the tide under his stern.

He therefore had the engines running at three-quarter throttle. In case of any further accidents, two boys took it in turns to stand by in the engine-room to ' help ' Mr McCann.

Though unable to prove anything at all after his talk with the engineer, Captain Drew was certain that the events of the previous afternoon were not quite such an accident as he was supposed to believe. McCann had been eloquent—too eloquent, he felt. He had provided an answer for everything. Well, the man might be in the clear, the skipper thought, but he simply couldn't take chances.

By the rail Robin stood having a breath of fresh air before turning in. He was terribly worried about the way things were going, but felt that there was so little he could do at the moment. He was a bit shaken by the afternoon's excitement and his arms ached terribly. Still, he had the satisfaction of knowing that his duty had been well done. He had not failed the others when his help was needed.

Before he was aware of it, Timothy Ballard was at his side. Robin looked up and smiled.

' Hullo, Timothy,' he said as he straightened up. ' Just off to turn in. We're on the graveyard watch, 12.00 to 4.00 a.m., you know.'

The other put a hand on his shoulder. 'Hang on a moment, Robin,' he asked. 'I would like to have a chat if you can spare a few minutes. Shan't take long—honestly.'

Robin had been dreading this. Ever since he had been briefed by the skipper, he had managed to avoid long talks with anyone, even Timothy. Recently he felt that Ballard had suspected that something was wrong. If questioned, Robin just didn't know what to say. He couldn't lie to his friend, and yet he was under a promise not to reveal the true nature of his undertaking.

'Let it wait till morning,' he pleaded. 'I'll feel fresher then.'

Timothy dropped his hand, but stood blocking the way.

'I told the lads I would try to see you,' he replied. 'But, of course, it can wait.'

Robin felt a cold shiver run down his spine. So they knew, or at any rate suspected something, he thought. The question was—how much?

He turned as if to go. 'All right,' he said. 'Just do what you——'

'Hang on, Robin. Can I say something first?'

'Go ahead.'

'I have thought a good deal about this, and it is not easy to say; that's why I want to get it off my chest. As I see it, something is wrong. We have no idea what it is, but strange things have taken place, you can't deny that, while you yourself have been sort of moody and preoccupied. You have avoided all of us and just now you wanted to get out of talking to me alone. We all trust you, Robin. If something is not straight then I know that you would have told us right away. Since you haven't, then I think you can't be allowed to—for some reason or other. To ask questions wouldn't be fair.'

'No,' he went on as Robin was about to protest, 'don't interrupt me. Am I right in my reasoning? If I am, what do you want us to do—because we are right behind you, Robin, every inch of the way.'

Suddenly Robin felt terribly relieved. He had been dreading this meeting with Timothy, yet he knew that sooner or later it had to come. Now, thanks to the real understanding of his friend, he saw just what he must do. For a moment he couldn't reply. When he recovered, he answered slowly.

'You are right. There is something which I am not allowed to discuss with anyone. Captain Drew made me promise before we left Darroch. As for the various mishaps which seem to have dogged us since we left—I don't know—honestly I don't. They may be due to chance—they may not.'

While he had been speaking he had been thinking hard. Now his mind was made up.

'I'll tell you what to do, Timothy,' he said. 'Keep your eyes and ears skinned. Tell me if you notice anything suspicious, and above all prevent stupid rumours from getting about. Look, I must go now. I don't want to be seen hanging around with people more than I can help. You'll do as I ask?'

'Rely on me, Robin. We will all be ready if you need us.'

Trenchard hurried below.

Chapter X

ALL BUT SUNK

The following day broke fine and clear, though the wind remained high. Drew had succeeded in catching the tide which now helped them past the island of Scarba towards the Sound of Jura. It had been a rough night with little enough sleep for anyone, nor had the navigation been particularly easy. The lighthouses were working but on reduced brilliance which limited their range. In addition, their characteristic flashings had been altered for security reasons, and though Naval Control supplied a key it was no easy matter to pick up and identify a strange light on an unknown coast.

Things had gone well, however, and now all hands were on deck as the Gulf of Corryvreckan, between Scarba and Jura, came abeam to starboard. As they passed the opening, Rees told the boys of the dreaded whirlpool and the ships it had claimed in former years.

Looking at the stretch of water, so pleasant in the morning sun, they could well believe the stories, for there was a sinister air about it which made them glad to pass on to the island, or rather the rock, of Ruadh Sgeir which lay right in the middle of the Sound to the south-west of Ardnoe Point and the entrance to the Crinan Canal. Jackie knew the canal well, all the way to Ardrishaig. He had a host of amusing stories about the times when he had been through in his father's boat, and he loved to tell of the jams caused by the fair-weather sailors in their power craft and white yachting caps.

Venturer bowled along, making good distance, and in a few hours she was abeam of the Paps of Jura on the southern end of the island. Though not high, these hills stand out conspicuously from the surrounding country, making an excellent landmark for sailors.

The day passed pleasantly enough, without incident. Towards evening it was possible to pick out, with the help of the glasses, the island of Rathlin lying dead ahead, behind it the coast of Northern Ireland and, to port, the dark mass of the Mull of Kintyre.

As they turned south and east towards the entrance to the North Channel, they lost the protection of the island of Islay. The long rollers from the Atlantic caught the ship under the starboard quarter to send her cork-screwing forward through the white-capped seas. It was the same motion which they had experienced on clearing the Firth of Lorne, and it claimed a few victims within a very short space of time, sending them scurrying to the lee rail.

Before turning in, the Captain had mustered all hands aft to remind them they were now crossing the busy shipping lanes. He demanded extra alertness from the look-outs and a general tightening up of ship's discipline all round.

It was as well he did so, for that very night the schooner was all but rammed by a fast merchantman which appeared to have come either from Larne or Belfast and which was evidently on its way to the Clyde.

Eight bells had just sounded for the change of the watch at four a.m. The duty crew were standing about drinking their cocoa while the watch below were making tracks for a warm bunk with all possible speed. Rees had handed over the ship to Howarth in the usual way. 'Course S.E. both engines off'—as it seemed fairly certain that they would be able to catch the tide round the next headland, the Mull of Galloway—'Sails set ; fore, main and staysail. Ships in sight : a steam vessel well out, four points on the starboard bow.'

Having made his report, Rees bade his relief good night and went below. The ship settled down. Howarth checked the course, engine speed and set of the sails. The wind had altered a little, so he had the boys take in the sheets on all sails to trim her better. The steaming lights and masthead light of the approaching ship were altering their bearing, relative to the schooner, rapidly. That meant she was coming up fast.

Howarth looked to see that their own lights were in order. Both port and starboard lamps were burning brightly and, being a sailing ship, she carried no masthead light. By the rule of road it was the duty of the steamer to give way to sailing ships. The schooner, for her part, was obliged to 'maintain her course and speed'.

Satisfied that all was well, the bos'n told Trenchard to keep a look-out while he went in to examine the chart in case there were any 'alter courses' due during the watch. Robin took the night glasses and focused them on the approaching ship.

She was a fair size ; just below 10,000 tons, he thought, by the vague outline which he could see.

She was deep in the water, pushing a small mountain of white foam ahead of her with her blunt stem.

Robin looked at her for a couple of minutes then quickly called the bos'n.

'What's wrong, lad?' asked Howarth as he came up blinking in the darkness after the white light of the chart-room.

'I don't think she has seen us, sir,' said Robin.

'Nonsense,' the older man said. 'He will see us all right. He'll be altering course to port to pass under our stern in a moment. Here, give me the glasses.'

Robin passed them over. For a full minute there was silence, then Howarth suddenly rapped out: 'Call the Captain—quick!'

Drew seemed to sleep with one ear and an eye open. As soon as the whistle on the voice-pipe by his ear sounded, he was on his feet. Ten seconds later he was on the deck. A quick look was enough.

'Sound the general alarm. Call all hands, Trenchard.'

As Robin sprang to obey, the Captain turned to the bos'n. 'The boy's right. He hasn't seen us. With this wind on our quarter we haven't a hope of pulling up. If we try to alter course he may do the same and then we'll have a real pile-up. No, we must stand on. Take the mainsail off her, quickly.'

'Aye, aye, sir. Stand by main throat and peak halyards. Clear for lowering!' Howarth bellowed.

By this time the whole crew were on deck, life-jackets inflated. Rees got the foghorn going while Drew flashed the Aldis lamp to attract attention. As the ropes began to race through the sheaves,

Drew turned to McCann, one of the first to appear from below.

'Take over the foghorn from Rees and just keep it going,' he snapped. 'Mr Rees, attend to the sail.'

'I must go below to get——' McCann began saying.

'You'll do what you are told in double quick time!' Drew thundered. 'Jump to it, man.'

Rees thrust the handle of the machine into the engineer's grasp. 'Now it's winding like mad you'll have to be,' he shouted, and vanished into the mound of canvas.

As the wailing note struck up from the box, Drew smiled grimly. At least I know where you are, he thought. But there was no time to lose. The huge mass of steel, ploughing relentlessly on towards them, could be seen through the darkness, while the air vibrated to the throb of her powerful engines.

In spite of all their efforts, there was no sign of life aboard her. Everyone on *Venturer* stood petrified when the truth dawned upon them. They were going to be rammed!

'All hands aft!' Drew's voice rang out loud and clear. 'Stand by to gybe.'

With mainsail off her, the schooner had lost way, but it was still touch and go whether she could escape intact. The moon broke through the clouds, bathing everything in a thin, watery light as *Venturer* slid down into the trough of a deep wave. High above them the crew of the smaller boat saw the huge anchors in their pipes, the rows of portholes and the white streak where the merchantman's condenser water poured out over the side like a waterfall.

Venturer rose on the next wave, and those who watched imagined it was for the last time, for surely she must smash her bowsprit against the grey steel plates abeam of the monster's engine-room. As she began to lift, Drew spun the wheel hard over to starboard. The sudden application of the rudder together with the upward motion made the schooner pause. The wind backed the sails, causing her to gybe, while the fore boom and headsail sheets lashed wildly over on to the new tack, almost tearing the preventers from the deck.

It was a dangerous thing to do but the only one. The sudden rush of wind into the foresail forced the ship over till her scuppers were right under. Both sail and cordage were new, however, and they stood the strain without splitting. The manoeuvre succeeded, since in the time taken for her to change tack, the cargo ship tore past, missing her by feet—if not inches!

In a matter of seconds it was all over. The massive counter of the steamer was swallowed up in the gloom, while only the diminishing noise of her engines proved that the whole thing had not been a bad dream.

Captain Drew was a wise man. Badly shaken as he was himself, he knew that the best cure for nerves was work.

'Stand by to go about,' he ordered. 'Mr Howarth, Mr Rees and Mr McCann attend to the fore sheet. I'll bring her round gently. Haul in the slack and take a turn. When the gybe is complete, ease out again. Trenchard, take the headsails. All ready? Lee helm. Gybe—oh.'

No sooner was she steadied on the new tack than

he gave the order ' Up mainsail '. All hands tailed on to the ropes, heaving hard as the heavy spar climbed slowly up the mast.

Finally all was shipshape again ; sails set, ropes coiled neatly on belaying-pins. All hands settled down to a mug of steaming cocoa and over it discussed how close a shave they had experienced. As Mr Rees remarked, one could understand now how people in lifeboats or upon rafts were missed in spite of having seen a ship and set off rockets to attract attention.

Chapter XI

A NIGHT OF STORM

Before leaving Darroch, Captain Drew had made the crew shift quite a large amount of the ship's ballast. The result of this was to improve her trim. But even so she was still at her best with a good breeze on her quarter. Once for'ard of the beam she found it hard to work to windward and when, as now, both wind and tide were against her, she made little good ground at all.

For the better part of the day, it seemed, they had tacked back and forward between Belfast Lough and the Mull of Galloway. Each time she approached the land the boys looked ashore, hoping that at last they had rounded the point, and each time they were disappointed as the bluff rose ahead, leaving them no option but to put about once again towards the Irish coast.

At first it had been a strong wind which had headed them, proving too much for the combined efforts of sail and engines. But now with the onset of darkness, the tide had joined forces with the gale, with the result that they had no hope of winning through till slack water anyway, and then only if the wind shifted a point or two as well.

Midnight passed with little change, but it was not till about three in the morning that Rees noticed a shift of wind.

'She'll come up a bit, mister,' he called to Neil Townrow, who was on the wheel. 'Let her come round to south-east.'

'South-east she is, sir,' Neil reported as he checked on the new course.

'Very good—steady.'

'Steady, sir.'

The rough weather had whipped up a nasty swell in the Irish Sea, and *Venturer* had taken a hard hammering as she tried to force her way south. Everything was straining with the motion, and even the helmsman was having difficulty in holding the ship to within ten degrees either side of her course. Rees went aft to him.

'Now, 'ow you getting on, lad?' he asked. ''Aving a bit of a job 'olding her to it, I'll wager.'

'Yes, sir,' Neil replied. 'She keeps falling off badly as each wave strikes her.'

'Well now, you don't want to be always peering into that compass and 'urting your eyes more than necessary. It's a fine sky, though the wind's 'igh. Put her dead on course, then pick a star clear of the end of the bowsprit. They move slowly in the sky, so you can steer on them for quite a while. Go on—try it. After twenty minutes or 'arf an hour you check it again with the compass.'

Neil steadied her right on the south-east.

'There you are,' Rees continued, 'See that bright star ahead? Steer on that. What's it's name? Now *you* ought to know it.'

Neil didn't—and said so.

'Goodness me!' Rees threw up his hands in mock despair. 'And you call yourself a seaman!' He pointed upwards. 'Look up there. See that great white band across the sky? That's the Milky Way. Our star is over there, at the corner of the rectangle. Got it? Good. Now if you look carefully you'll see three stars close together about the middle of the figure, and what looks like a short line of stars hangs down from them. That's *Orion.* The four corners are his shoulders and feet; the rest represents his belt with sword attached. You're steering on one of his shoulders, *Betelgeux.* The other stars are *Bellatrix,* and *Rigel.*'

'Good!' exclaimed Neil. 'I've often heard of Orion, but I never knew the names of the various stars.'

'When you've been at sea as long as I have, my lad, you'll get chummy with them,' Rees observed. 'They're easy to pick up on a clear night when you can see them all; the *Plough,* with the *Pole Star* lying off the pointers and the semicircle of *Capella, Castor, Pollux, Procycon,* and *Sirius,* the Dog Star.

'But it's when you can only catch a glimpse of one or two through a rent in a storm cloud that you have to keep your wits about you. Take an observation of the wrong star, work it up into a longitude and you could be miles off course. Now I remember once——'

He never finished what he was going to say. Suddenly the schooner took a terrific crack at a wave which all but stopped her in her tracks. She shuddered from stem to stern. There was a cry from below.

'Quick—call the watch, the wooden plug in the pantry has come right out and water is pouring in!'

Rees sprinted for'ard, vanishing down the ladder with remarkable agility for a man his age. Already there was a good deal of water inboard, while every time the ship drove deep into a wave it fountained up like a fire hydrant, hitting the deckhead and filling the small space with a fine mist. The force behind the jet was considerable, as Rees discovered when he tried to replace the wood during a brief lull.

Just as he had it in place the forefoot struck the next sea with the result that the plug was blasted from his grasp to ricochet round the room from bulkhead to bulkhead. In an instant he was soaked. He tried again with no better success, and all the time the water level was rising. This was serious.

'Call the Captain and Mr Howarth,' he said, wiping the salt water from his hair. 'Form a chain and start bailing where the water is lying in the after end there. Send a man to rig the bilge pumps. Tell him to look quick about it.' Rees was well and truly drenched, and the water felt freezing cold.

Howarth arrived with the Captain in next to no time. Drew took one look at the situation through the half-open door of the pantry.

'Apart from the seriousness of the leak,' he said, 'a large part of our stores are awash, so we'll be on short rations till we reach Anglesey. Trenchard?'

'Yes, sir.'

'Get into your bathing costume, double quick—get in there and see what you can do.'

'Aye, aye, sir.' Robin dodged off into the saloon to change.

'Mr Howarth, take charge on deck. Keep an eye on the pumping. Sound the bilge and keep me informed if the water is gaining on us. Mr Rees, get changed at once.'

'But, sir——'

'Don't argue. The youngsters are more able to stand this than you. Trenchard will do the job well.

You've done your bit, so off you go. Ballard ? Strip and assist Trenchard. Both of you will be needed there.'

'Very good, sir.'

'Chester ? '

'Sir ? ' He ran up at once.

'My regards to the engineer. Ask him to bring a bag of tools here at once.'

'Yes, sir.' Chester hurried away.

As the Captain finished his orders, Robin appeared ready for his attempt. He glanced at Drew's grim face which plainly told him that McCann would be better off where everyone could see him.

'All ready, Trenchard ? '

'Yes, sir.'

'Right. Take these spare wedges in with you; also the hammer. Get the hole plugged quickly as possible, then secure this plank over the top and fix both ends to the side battens. Off you go.'

Robin waded in. The Captain turned just in time to confront McCann, model of assistance, now arrived with his bag of tools. Since his last encounter with the Captain he had apparently been lying very low. After the incident with the engines he had made himself so affable to everyone, especially the bos'n and his mate, that Drew began to wonder whether he had misjudged the man. But he was not going to take any chances.

Up on deck, Howarth had put the ship about so that she was once again headed out towards the Irish coast. After the near accident with the merchantman, the look-outs had been doubled. Each now stood peering out into the darkness, alert for any thickening in the general gloom ahead which might materialise into solid form. The wind was keen, causing their eyes to water with strain and fatigue.

Below deck Ballard and Trenchard were battling with the geyser which roared up from the planking each time they struck a wave. Twice they had succeeded in placing the wedge, but before they could secure it the force of water had blown it out, hosing them down in the process.

Through the bulkhead they were treated to a running commentary on what to do and how to do it. The water was sloshing about more than ankle deep and both boys were shivering in spite of their exertions.

'Water gaining on us now, sir!' That was the bos'n shouting down the after companion-way.

Drew heard the report, pondered for a moment before banging on the bulkhead.

'Trenchard!' he called. 'Can you continue a bit longer?'

'Yes, sir.'

'Carry on, then. I am going to check away the sheets and take her right off the wind; then with the breeze almost aft the seas will roll up under her counter, so you will have a better chance of repairing the damage without the added difficulty of the vessel driving into a head sea.'

'Very good, sir. We'll manage it then.'

The duty watch were piped, the manoeuvre carried out, and when the *Venturer* was heading back up the Irish Sea with the wind astern of her, Robin and Timothy made one more effort at curing the leak.

As soon as they felt a wave roll away from the keel, they rammed home the peg, belting it soundly with the mallet before the following one should dislodge it. When the stern post rose once more the water sprayed out but less violently this time. Again the mallet did its work and again the leak was less pronounced. This continued until no water came in, and even then they gave it a few hefty welts for good luck.

Since starting the job the two boys, although soaking wet, had been too engrossed to notice that they were almost blue with cold. They could have worked in sea boots, oilskins and sou'westers, but this would have taken time to put on, and also have been a hindrance in the confined space.

'Water going down now, sir.' It was Howarth reporting again.

'Very good,' the Captain replied. 'Keep the pumps going till she is dry again. How's it looking inside there?'

'I think we've succeeded,' Robin called back through the bulkhead. 'The inboard end of the bar has been made fast, sir, and Ballard is screwing down the outboard side. Another couple of minutes and we will be ready for the mopping-up squad.'

'Good lads.' Drew sounded very relieved. 'Well done. Have a brew of cocoa ready in the galley for them when they come out, Mr McCann. Inspect the job, strengthen it if necessary and let me know when everything is squared up.'

'Very good, sir.'

'Captain Drew?' Mr Rees came up puffing and out of breath.

'Yes?'

'There is a convoy dead ahead making up channel. From their steaming lights I would say there are about thirty ships in all.'

'I'll come up.'

After the leak had been plugged, *Venturer* had been put about once more and was now heading straight towards the oncoming vessels.

'Lights burning brightly?'

'Aye, sir, burning brightly,' Rees replied.

'Good, then we stand on.' Drew looked through the glasses. 'We should sail right between the lines as we go now.'

'That's about it.' The bos'n's mate sounded anything but enthusiastic.

The lights were some distance off, however, and the Captain saw no point in worrying. Steam gives way to sail, he thought, therefore we carry on. Anyway, as things now stood there was hope at last of getting clear of the Mull so that every cable made good was vital.

'We'll keep her going, helmsman, as close to the wind as you can.'

'Aye, aye, sir.'

'Tell the watch below to get turned in again and get some sleep.'

The message reached Robin and Timothy in the galley. They needed no second bidding after their ordeal, being only too glad to crawl into a warm bunk.

But no-one was to be comfortable for long. Peace had hardly settled over the ship when the look-out called excitedly: 'Searchlights fine on the port bow, sir.'

Those on deck looked in the direction of the

bearing. There they were, long silvery pencils of light inquisitively probing the sky, crossing and re-crossing like a pale version of the Northern Lights. As they watched, orange-yellow balls appeared on the ground, but before the boys could ask Rees what they were, the air was shaken by the thunder of bombs. Rees took a hurried look at the convoy, now less than a mile or so away.

'Call the Captain, quickly,' he ordered.

No sooner had he spoken than every light on the merchantmen went out as if operated by some unseen master switch. *Venturer* was left sailing at a good six knots straight into the heart of the now blacked-out convoy, while on shore one of the first raids on Barrow-on-Furness developed before their astounded eyes.

It was a terrifying sight and one which every man on board was destined to find stamped on his memory for ever after. Though still some forty miles away, the holocaust seemed to be so near that with little imagination the boys thought they could even feel the heat. As each plane let fall its deadly cargo, it swung out over the sea, passing directly above the ships.

The Captain took in the situation at a glance. Once again all hands were mustered on deck, each wearing his lifejacket and the protective red light which would be switched on before abandoning ship, should the necessity arise.

Look-outs were doubled once more, each warned to report loud and clear as soon as he saw anything approaching. Howarth took the wheel, Mr Rees positioned himself right for'ard, Robin and Timothy were placed one to port, the other to starboard amidships, leaving the skipper free to move about the deck.

As stick upon stick of high explosive crashed down upon the target, tension steadily mounted aboard the schooner. Though previous events had proved ugly at the time, no-one was foolish enough to underestimate the danger now threatening.

A German bomber pulled out of its dive scarcely more than mast high above the water. The air was filled with the pulsating throb of its engines—that curious noise which identified the enemy raiders as they tried to outwit our direction-finding gear. For a brief instant its ghastly black shape could be seen against the pale sky before it climbed for another run in. Above the din Robin heard the call from the bow look-out.

'Ship very fine on the port bow, sir.' He repeated the message to the Captain.

'Thank you. Starboard ten degrees, Mr Howarth.

'Starboard ten, sir.'

Minutes later the low outline of a huge tanker slid past less than a cable's length away. Her screw, deep buried beneath the surface, churned up a white line of phosphorescence astern of her. Drew was studying it closely, gauging the course of the convoy, when he received a further report.

'Ship dead ahead to starboard, sir.'

'Very good. Port easy.'

'Port easy, sir.'

'Let me know when she is three points on the bow.'

There was a pause ; then, 'Bearing three points, sir.'

'Right. Steady, helmsman.'

'Steady, sir.'

Captain Drew reckoned they were now heading straight between the rows of steamers. Another cable's length away—this time to starboard—a huge Blue Funnel cargo ship churned past, well down to her marks. Though the convoy had doused their lights in order to avoid attracting the unwelcome attention of aircraft, *Venturer* still carried her steaming lights. No plane would be likely to waste time on a lone sailing ship, but on the other hand it did warn the big ships of her presence.

Looking aft Robin could see Drew's face in the pale light of the binnacle. He marvelled how relaxed he appeared, how utterly in command of the situation. His orders were crisp and clear, and their tone brooked no delay in execution. Robin admired his Captain very much and his thoughts might have gone on long enough but for the sound of another bomber swinging out low from the coast.

Everyone peered up into the darkness in the direction of the throbbing engine note when suddenly the whole ship was flooded with light. Instinctively shielding their eyes against the unexpected glare, the crew of the *Venturer* saw the plane, its wing and tail a mass of flames, plunging straight towards them like a huge fire-ball launched by the gods.

CHAPTER XII

THE HEAD GOES AGROUND

IT was not only the immediate situation that caused Mr McCann to be scared. There were other fears and misgivings ; the prolonged spell at sea, for instance. He had not bargained for that. A trip down the Canal—yes, that had been expected ; but this continual tacking back and forth got on one's nerves, especially at night as he lay tossing in his bunk, unable to sleep, listening to the eerie whistle of the wind through the rigging, conscious of the terrifying proximity of the dark, cruel sea only a few feet away. These things were disturbing to a man with an uneasy mind. Not that McCann was afraid of tight situations, provided they were of his own making and he held the upper hand ; but the series of narrow escapes recently experienced had badly shaken him. Why hadn't he finished the job at Oban or, at least, within twenty-four hours of having left there ?

But there was something else which worried the engineer. When he took on the job he had only reckoned with the adults on board the *Venturer*. With regard to the Captain, whose rank placed him in a different and rather more difficult category than that of the crew, McCann considered he had played his part successfully. At the worst, he could only have aroused some curiosity, and felt confident that his latest efforts at 'cameraderie' had laid those two particular ghosts, the bos'n and his mate. Well, they were good chaps, but limited in intelligence, hard-working, dull and without a suspicion of that sharpness of wit which would have warned them that the engineer was not all that he appeared to be.

But the boys, whom earlier he had despised and mentally assigned to the care of their mothers' arms, were getting him down. Always courteous to him and ready volunteers for any sort of job, they were at times a little bit *too* polite for his peace of mind. It was their eyes which worried him. They held his gaze with never a falter, staring straight at him as though they could read his innermost thoughts.

Though he had tried hard to win them over, he never felt that they really accepted him. At first, he had laughed at the idea of being put off by a ' boatload of kids '. Now he knew that their dedication to the task, their determination never to give in or let their friends down whatever the cost and, worse still, the feeling that deep down the crew despised him for his own lack of guts—this was driving him mad. He must get his hands on those plans at once, and end this nightmare—or go under. This he knew for certain.

The thought had barely flitted across his mind when the bomber exploded above the ship, flooding the deck with orange light. For one terrible second he thought it must surely impale itself on the topmast, so low did it appear as it hurtled through the air trailing volumes of black smoke astern of it. The landing wheels stuck out at a crazy angle, the rudder hung over to one side while the port wing, severed by the force of the explosion, floated down on its own in a graceful spiral of fiery beauty to crash into the sea between two of the merchant ships to port.

The flaming wreckage did miss the schooner but it could only have been by a matter of feet. There was a roar and a splash as it plunged into the sea astern of *Venturer*, leaving a spreading circle of burning fuel on the water. The fuselage broke up under the impact to sink immediately and so far as those on board could see, nothing moved in the oily inferno which marked the grave of the men who had flown the plane.

It was war, however, and neither the sailing ship nor the convoy stopped to investigate the scene of the crash. As she passed the place, the corvette working astern of the big ships, acting as both rear guard and hospital ship, would make a search for survivors, but their chances were mighty thin.

That the German had missed the ships beneath was a miracle. Had it been guided by radio it could not have 'ditched' in a safer place, so far as the seamen were concerned. As for the pilot and crew of the plane, as Howarth said, though no-one liked to see men perish, that same plane had just dropped its bombs on Barrow, killing goodness knows how many women and children.

Once again the watch below turned in, hoping to salvage some sleep from the wreck of the night that was almost past. The crew were on for four hours and off for four—double watches as they are called—so that despite the interruptions and excitement, the men below came again on deck at eight bells—8 a.m. prompt. It was hard for the younger boys ; Drew knew that they were beginning to feel the strain.

After the suspense of the crash two had been

sick through sheer fatigue and reaction. But neither had reported the fact; they had gone back on watch to carry on with their jobs. The Captain was proud of the lads. He admired their determination and the way they kept their heads, carrying on with no heroics nor desire to win the limelight. Most of all he liked the way Trenchard handled them. They almost worshipped him, and little wonder, for he was just what a senior boy ought to be—though they were few and far between. Drew had admired their Headmaster for organising the trip before he left Darroch.

Now, even without the added danger of the plans, he wondered if the whole thing had been wise. The Head was no seaman and Drew could not help wondering whether he really understood the perils of the sea when he committed the boys to his care.

Venturer cleared the convoy without further incident, though once or twice they came uncomfortably close to some of the huge grey shapes as they passed down the line.

Throughout the following day and night the wind continued to blow strong from the south, again leaving the Captain no option but to tack down the Irish Sea past Blackpool and Southport towards Anglesey and the entrance to the Menai Straits.

On the morning of the second day after the raid, the wind died away to a flat calm, the sun blazed out and on a sea of glass *Venturer* motored up the narrow channel towards Beaumaris.

Long before they saw the training ship *Conway*, they passed her cadets out in their boats, rowing with care and precision under the eye of a senior hand. As they came abeam of the wonderful old ship they saluted her before going on to drop anchor farther up. The hook was hardly on the bottom when a boat shot out from the main gangway of the *Conway* carrying her Captain together with Dr Dreaver, the Headmaster of St Mark's. The whaler closed the *Venturer*, making to come alongside. The helmsman, a tall lad in cap, uniform and brass buttons, gave his orders loud and clear. The crew, also in uniform, were well trained and determined to put up a good show. They did so, laying the narrow craft by the pilot ladder with hardly the need of a fender.

Looking down at them the St Mark's boys felt pretty scruffy. Though all had washed and squared up on the run in, they were still badly in need of a bath, hair was matted, hands ingrained with salt and dirt.

The rigours of the past thirty-six hours had taken toll of what passed for uniform—blue high-necked sweaters and heavy blue trousers. The result was a motley looking lot in bits and pieces of every imaginable colour of clothing. No wonder they felt like poor relations beside the beautifully kept boats of the training ship.

But they need not have worried, for when they got to know the *Conway* lads better they found out how much they envied the St Mark's boys. As one of them said: 'We learn navigation, signalling, small boat work and the rest, but you chaps are seamen. You have sailed your ship from Darroch to Beaumaris. What does it matter what you look like? We would give our eye-teeth to accomplish a tenth of what you have done.'

They were a grand crowd of boys, good hosts who made friends easily with the lads from the *Venturer*. Though neither lot knew it at the time, they were laying the foundations of an association which was to bind the two schools together right through the war.

Dr Dreaver was an active man for his age, but his build was very much against him when it came to scaling pilot ladders. Always with an eye open for a good chance, Chester had torn himself away from his precious maps to have a quick whip-round the ship, laying bets whether or not the Head would fall in the drink on his way aboard. In point of fact he nearly did.

Just as he got one foot on the bottom rung of the ladder, the wash from a passing launch caused the whaler to move out from the schooner's side. Dr Dreaver was in imminent danger of performing the splits and would most certainly have fallen in but for the swift action of the bow and stern men who hauled the craft in again so that his second foot could get a hold. It was a ticklish moment, but it passed.

His safety, however, was short lived, for Dr Dreaver was bubbling over with enthusiasm which led him to fuss about all over the ship, determined to see everything and everyone on her. It suddenly dawned on him that he had not seen Trenchard, though he had been aboard for nearly a quarter of an hour.

'I think everything is wonderful, Captain Drew, simply wonderful,' he said. 'But where is Trenchard? I have not seen a sign of him yet.'

'He is below, Dr Dreaver,' the skipper replied,

'squaring off the chain locker. He'll be up shortly.'

'Wonderful,' repeated the Head, using his favourite expression for the umpteenth time. 'I'll just go down and see him.'

With this, his huge form bore down on the small hatch and steep, narrow companion-way to the lower deck. Before Drew or anyone else could stop him he had manoeuvred himself stern first into the opening and was already commencing his descent.

Down below, Robin was trying to clean out the chain locker. The boards, which in reality were the deck of the galley, were all up, exposing the cavity which housed the anchor cables when not in use.

Being in a strong tideway, Drew had *Venturer* lying to both anchors, each having a long drift of cable so that the space below the deck was fairly empty. Since the cables had been frequently used during the trip, the locker was fouled by heavy clods of mud and clay together with other rubbish picked up by the links on the dirty bottom and subsequently hauled inboard. The stuff stank, and having the consistency of black, oily porridge, cleaning it up was no joke. As he worked, Robin found the light from above suddenly cut off. Without looking up, he called out :

'Oh, for goodness' sake, shift your great frame out of the light, can't you ! This job is bad enough without trying to do it in the dark.'

Evidently the culprit couldn't or wouldn't hear him, so Robin put down his shovel, straightened his back and prepared to give the intruder an earful : 'Look here, you great jelly fish, get your massive—'

The words died away and he spluttered into silence on glancing up to recognise instantly the impressive mass of his Headmaster—even if the viewpoint was a little unusual.

'Sir, I'm terribly sorry. I thought——'

'Delighted to see you, my dear boy.'

Dr Dreaver, his head still on a level with the upper deck, was only vaguely aware of someone below speaking to him. He managed to ease himself down another couple of rungs of the ladder.

'Be with you in a moment,' he boomed.

The awful truth of what was about to happen dawned on the Captain and Robin simultaneously. Both started shouting advice at the same time, the one from above and the other from beneath. Because the opening was so narrow, the Headmaster's body filled it completely, with the result that the skipper did not hear Robin, nor Robin the skipper. What was worse, in the general confusion Dr Dreaver heard neither. Preoccupied with the operation of pushing himself through something resembling a filter funnel, he pressed on regardless.

Some people seem bound by fate to do the wrong thing when they board a vessel. Ashore, they may be astute, clever men, but once clear of Mother Earth and with a fathom or two of water beneath their keel a jinx seems to beset them. Whatever can go wrong—and there is so much on a ship—goes wrong. They fall over the mushroom vents on deck, get one leg caught up in coils of rope, find their new suits covered in grease from the windlass and invariably cause the hair on the bos'n's neck to rise like a worried mongrel's by referring to the bow as the sharper of the two ends. Dr Dreaver was such a man. On land his knowledge of boats was average. Once afloat, however, he was completely adrift. Whatever he did seemed certain to go wrong somehow, and he rarely got off any of the School boats without another story joining the already large collection which circulated in St Mark's and which was jealously guarded, to be handed down to following generations, suitably embellished.

'Sir, please stop! There is no plank beneath.'

'Yes, I know it is rather dank down there,' called the Head.

'Sir, stop.'

'What's rot? I don't understand. Ugh! That's better. Got one shoulder down now, there we are.'

The time for talk was past. In desperation Robin seized one of the galley floorboards, whipped it over the opening directly where the Head's foot should have landed as it left the bottom rung. But it was not to be. Relieved to have made it, Dr Dreaver ducked to get his head clear of the hatch combing, took a large pace astern and pushed off with both arms. Seconds later he was flat on his back on the bottom of the chain locker in several inches of evil-smelling glue with Robin peering anxiously down from above.

It was a stroke of good fortune that the Head was unhurt. Though the distance from the foot of the ladder to the bottom of the locker was only about three feet six inches, Dr Dreaver was a heavy man and could well have broken a bone. His safety might have been due to Robin's catching his coat and so helping to break the fall.

The Head made a brave effort to scramble to his feet, but unfortunately had reckoned without the steep slope of the locker sides. Being right up near the bow, the hull came in sharply towards the keel. His feet slipped and down he went again with a bump !

Robin understood the gravity of the situation, but the sight of his Headmaster sprawling helplessly in the filth and slime of the cable locker proved too much for his sense of humour to resist. Unable to suppress the desire, he began to laugh, a gentle and restrained laugh at first, which soon broke out in a low chuckle ; then all at once he was doubled up with gales of laughter, the tears coursing down his cheeks.

The more he tried to heave the Head up the more they both slipped and floundered in the mire, and Robin, his strength ebbing with mirth, was powerless to do anything about it.

Luckily at that moment Timothy Ballard came through the saloon door and between them the boys hauled the unfortunate man to his feet. To begin with he was anything but amused, but when he learned that he had been warned and how Robin had tried to save him, he softened enough to see the funny side of it.

His suit was ruined but he refused to change or borrow fresh clothes. They rowed him ashore where his car whisked him off to the hotel. But in an hour he was aboard again demanding to hear more about the trip, while he went from boy to boy assuring himself that no-one was the worse for the voyage.

Chapter XIII

GRAVE SUSPICION

That evening, their first anchored off Beaumaris, all hands were enjoying a hot cup of cocoa before turning in early. Trenchard was being made to relate the story of Dr Dreaver and the adventure in the chain locker when Captain Drew came through the door from aft.

'Sit down, lads,' he said as the crew rose to their feet. 'You are all owed a good rest. You've worked hard and it hasn't all been fun either. Mr Howarth, Mr Rees and myself are proud of you. Keep it up, but remember it is not all over yet. Though we are past the worst of the shipping lanes, bad weather, engine failure or just plain ill luck could still make the last leg from Caernarvon to Aberdovey mighty unpleasant.'

He turned to Percy. 'What's this I hear about you not wanting to go to a dance tonight, Chester ?' he asked laughingly.

Percy went scarlet, to the accompaniment of hoots of laughter from his mates.

'It's not me, sir. I just took the message from *Conway* when she called up on the Aldis lamp. They wanted some of us to go ashore to some 'hop' but none of them would go. Said they were all too tired. Truth is, sir, none of 'em can dance.'

'Oh, I see.' Drew grinned. 'And you ?'

'Well, I can't show them up by going on my own. It wouldn't be very nice, if you know what I mean, would it, sir ?'

Drew raised a quizzical eyebrow in the direction of Jackie Main.

'That right?' he asked.

'Him,' Jackie scoffed. 'In a dance hall he is as manoeuvrable as a Thames barge, and about as elegant.'

This was greeted with howls of laughter as Chester made to attack his tormentor.

'Pipe down, you two; you will need all your energy for tomorrow.'

There was a sudden silence. The boys knew their Captain fairly well by now, well enough at any rate to realise that when he spoke as he was doing now it almost always heralded important news.

'What is happening, sir?' Ballard wanted to know.

'Feeling fit?' Drew suddenly countered.

Timothy was rather nonplussed. 'Yes—er—yes, sir,' he stammered. 'That is, I think so, sir. I'll be all right after a night's sleep,' he replied. Then rather slowly, 'Why, sir?'

'Lots of hard work to do.' Drew idly trimmed the wick of the oil lamp as it hung from the main beam.

'That's nothing new, sir,' Squeak Naylor cut in. 'We're almost used to it now.'

'Ah well, get a good night's sleep then. Nothing like it to build up the body, is there?' This to Mr Rees who had entered the saloon from for'ard.

'Nothing like it,' agreed the big Welshman. 'Indeed I feel like getting my head down too.'

'Come on, then,' the Captain said. 'We'll leave the lads to it.'

'But, sir, you haven't told us what all this sleep is in aid of,' Robin reminded him.

Half-way through the door the Captain paused, turned and stuck his head back into the saloon again.

'Why, neither I have,' he said, the serious note of his voice failing to conceal the twinkle in his piercing blue eyes. 'You have an athletics contest against the *Conway*, starting at 2.30 p.m. Good night.' And he was gone.

The bombshell raised wails of protest from all and sundry. The boys were furious and turned to vent their wrath on Mr Rees, who stood grinning all over his great face. But it was no use. The Head had arranged it the day before *Venturer* hove in sight, and that being so there was only one thing to do—get on with it.

The boys made their preparations, and if beaten in the overall competition, the verdict was in the balance right up to the final event—the mile.

After his talk with the Head of the School, Timothy had successfully quietened the curiosity of the rest of the crew and so, for the present, everything seemed safe and under control. The few days' respite were spent in re-storing ship and replacing much of the food spoiled by sea water when the vessel had sprung a leak in the pantry.

Robin asked Captain Drew whether he thought there would be any fresh danger from their enemies. They were sitting on the rail aft, one night when the rest of the crew were aboard the *Conway* watching a film show. It was a wonderful evening. After the bad weather the winds had fallen away, the air had become warm and the phosphorescence was so bright that it hurt the eyes.

As the small boat put out from the ship's side her six oars made a wonderful picture, each stroke flashing liquid fire when the blade struck the water. Even the drips as the boys feathered looked like luminous fireballs, while the water fell away from the stem in cascades of ghostly greenish light. All were quite excited by the spectacle, never having seen anything quite like it before.

'No,' said the Captain. 'Our friends won't try anything while we are here. There are too many people about; too much attention is centred on us. They will strike again when we are on our own, when they can make a quick get-away without fear of being found out too soon.'

Robin looked straight at his Captain. 'Sir, may I make a suggestion?'

Drew knocked his pipe out. 'Yes, lad; go ahead.'

'Well, the longer we stave them off the more desperate these fellows will become.'

'Yes.'

'Don't you think we could enlist the help of the bos'n and his mate, sir?'

Drew turned to gaze out for a few moments over the dark sea, then smiled wearily at Robin.

'Not a hope. I have tried them—very discreetly of course. They think McCann is marvellous. The fellow has won them over with, I suspect, cigarettes and goodness knows what else. No, Robin, short of telling them all—and that we cannot do—we must fight alone. I have also decided to say nothing to your Headmaster. I gave my word to the men up north, Professor Landsberger and the Commanding Officer of Spynie Aerodrome. Perhaps I was wrong, but no good ever came of changing horses in mid-stream. We must go on by ourselves to see this thing through.'

Two days later the schooner took leave of her kind hosts and nosed her way through the dangerous waters towards the castle and town of Caernarvon. As they waved farewell no-one could have foreseen that the gallant old ship was to end her days here, a victim of the unpredictable currents which daily flowed around and beneath her keel.

The trip down to Caernarvon had been made by engine, though at first the calm weather had broken about midday when the placid waters became ruffled by a strong wind once more.

Venturer slowed down as the pilot boat came alongside. She made fast with stout lines fore and aft, then together the two boats headed out towards the bar. The gaunt, granite walls of the ancient fortress fell away astern. Out ahead, the bow look-out could barely see the line of foam which marked the bar. Gulls flew around the masts filling the air with their mournful cries. After a brief spell of heat the breeze turned chilly again. To starboard, dark threatening clouds were forming up and their associated squalls were whipping the waves into white horses.

With the approach of the open water the motion increased. The seas were becoming short and steep, causing the schooner to behave like a rocking horse, pitching backwards or forwards in quick, hard jerks. They had been late enough in making the town. With the last of the ebb already flowing strongly, it was touch and go whether they could clear the bar before the young flood caught them in its grip.

With conditions as they were on arrival it had been a fair gamble. Now, however, with wind and sea in their teeth, the ship simply did not have the power to make it, even with the help of the pilot cutter lashed alongside. The bar buoy had shown up all right, but instead of coming abeam, it had become stuck about a point for'ard of that. The fact was they were not going ahead. Wind and tide had won—at least temporarily.

The pilot looked with some alarm at the conical buoy, then turned to the Captain. 'We'll never make it, sir. Better turn back now while we still have sea room. The Fishery Cruiser is going out on the morning tide. With a couple of tow ropes from her and my own boat lashed alongside we should make it even if the wind does stay where it is.'

'Very good, pilot. I'm sure you are right. It is disappointing, but there we are.'

Not everyone was downcast at the decision to return to Caernarvon for the night. Through the engine-room porthole McCann watched as they swung through three hundred and sixty degrees to head inland again and he smiled, an oily, self-satisfied smirk.

On a headland nearby, a tall figure in a black overcoat saw the unexpected turn and he, too, smiled. Plans had been laid at Beaumaris in a steamy, low-down tavern. This new move would allow of further consultation that very night. With luck, another twenty-four hours might see it all over. The engine purred into life, driving the black Alvis towards the town and a cheap hotel on the waterfront.

Drew anchored off the old fortress, sang down :

'Finished with engines,' and gave his orders to the bos'n for the night: 'Start heaving up 4.30 to-morrow morning, bos'n. Pilot is due at 5.00 together with the Fishery Cruiser. It is an early start, there will have to be no shore leave for anyone, so that we'll all have an early night.'

'Aye, aye, sir—a good idea.'

When McCann heard of the Captain's orders he was beside himself with rage. It was imperative that he reach the dingy hotel that evening, there to alter his scheme of operations for the following morning. The question was how could he do it without drawing suspicion or unwelcome attention on himself.

This stop was entirely unforeseen. All his engine-room stores had come aboard at Beaumaris so there was no use playing that one. All at once his rat-like face broke into a grin—a phone call to his ill mother! Chuckling, he set off to spin his line to the skipper.

Drew wasn't a captain for nothing. He and Robin had expected something like this to turn up and they were ready for him.

'So you have a phone call to make to your sick mother, Mr McCann? It is unfortunate that no-one will be going ashore. But we can get round that all right.' Drew smiled. 'What is her number?'

'Garscube 8721, sir.'

'Trenchard. Tell Naylor to call up the coast-guard station and have them put that number through on the two-way radio.'

The engineer's face went white with rage. 'I want to go ashore,' he demanded.

'Just to make a phone call which you can do from here,' said the Captain softly. 'Have you anything else you want to do perhaps?' Drew's eyes bored through the hapless man like smouldering coals.

'Yes—I mean no—oh, look, why can't I take the boat?'

'Because I say so. Any further questions?'

McCann took one look at his questioner and climbed down. He was a coward at heart and, like all cowards, he knew a better man when he saw one.

'Mr McCann's call, sir.' Squeak sang out from the set.

'Thank you. Carry on. It will cost you a little more, but I am sure it will be worth it.'

Still furious, the engineer took the instrument and phoned his Mum.

The incoming tide slackened, paused and at the first sign of the ebb *Venturer* started to swing round her anchor. McCann had been up most unusually late for him, busying himself with this and that, a turn on a nut here, a drop of oil there. No-one paid much attention to him at all.

Just as she was due to swing, however, he bustled up on deck and announced that he must give the steering gear a drop of oil in readiness for the following day. Rees thought it an odd thing to do, but let him go ahead. It took him some time. It seemed that something needed adjusting while the helm was hard a-port. Whatever it was, he finished it just as the ship started to swing, stern on, to the buildings of the town.

'Man,' he said, 'did ever you see the like of yon?

There's nae joy in the blue stern light. I'll hae tae fix it.'

For the next ten minutes or so the blue-coloured light flickered on and off while he scraped away at the wires trying to repair the faulty connections. You couldn't see the bulb from the deck unless you leaned far out over the counter. But ashore, from a dirty window in a filthy hotel room the message was seen, read and understood. One short flash on a green torch signified acknowledgement, and the devilish scheme was laid.

By five they were on their way to the entrance again. Two bow lines were made fast to the stern of the Fishery Cruiser and the pilot cutter secured alongside added her quota of power.

The strong winds of the previous evening had left a very heavy swell running so that as they approached the bar the motion between the three ships grew more violent with each cable's length gained. At one moment the hawsers would be hanging slack in the trough of the sea. The next instant they were whipped up taut as violin strings, trembling with vibration, their motion flinging off a spume of spray around them. With the bar buoy a half point for'ard of the beam it was clear to everyone that it would be touch and go again whether or not they won clear. Robin signalled to Timothy to lean over so that he could whisper to him.

'Timothy, I may need you soon. I have a hunch something is going to happen. Don't ask me what—I don't know. I want to stay here on these tow ropes. You see that the fore and main halyards are manned, ready for quick hoisting.

See also that someone stands by ready to cast off the pilot boat.'

'All right, but——'

'Never mind just now, there's a good chap.'

Just then McCann came up for'ard with his oil-can. 'I'll just put a drappie oil on they relieving tackles,' he mumbled, and bent over the ropes.

The next thing Robin knew there was a dreadful twang as the starboard tow line parted, the free end snaking away through the air like a thing alive. Before McCann had time to leap back the boy had reported.

'Starboard tow rope gone, sir.' As he spoke, *Venturer* threw herself up on the crest of a fresh roller. All the strain was taken by the one remaining line. It parted as well.

'Port line away, sir!'

There are times when true seamen know what to do without waiting for orders.

'Good luck, man.' The pilot slapped Drew on the arm, vaulted the rail into his launch to be cast off within seconds by the hands standing by.

Meantime the mainsail was inching its way up the mast, hauled by every man available. The angry teeth of the rocks to port were approaching fast. Would she—could she make it? The chances were a hundred to one against.

Drew spied the engineer sneaking below during the height of the turmoil. With a quick movement he barred his way, sending him for'ard again to heave on the ropes. Though his cabin was locked he had no intention of letting him loose. He was a slippery one, the same McCann. Once for'ard he waited a favourable opportunity before making for the fore hatch.

The main was set, the helm hard a-starboard, engines full ahead—with Howarth now standing by them on skipper's orders.

For the second time it seemed that *Venturer* must perish on the rocks. The pilot boat just managed to pull clear from the lee side. She now came up ahead and quickly passed a rope which Robin made fast to the bollard. This held the ship's head up while wind and engine drove the stern round. When they all but got clear, however, the keel struck a submerged rock. Fortunately, it was a rounded one with no jagged edges, and did not hole her, but the bump caused her to heel over at a crazy angle, while the gear below decks cascaded into a heap in the corner.

It seemed an eternity till she slid off the shelf. Inch by inch she started to sail, pulling away from the very jaws of death. A rapid check showed she was making no water.

Later, when all was safely set, Drew questioned Robin on the recent events.

'I'm sure McCann severed the first line, sir.'

'Yes, but can you prove it—did you see him?'

'No—not really, but I'm sure——'

'Maybe, maybe. We'll go below and discuss our next move.'

As he reached the foot of the ladder, the Captain stopped, astounded. His cabin door was wide open and all was in confusion.

CHAPTER XIV

MISSION COMPLETED

DREW surveyed the chaotic scene for a moment. 'Come in and shut the door,' he said.

Robin did so and Drew continued : 'Well, we are out of that one, and on the last leg home. If they—whoever *they* are—want the plans, then something will have to happen during the next twenty-four hours.'

'But'—Robin blurted out, 'I'm sure Mr McCann severed the tow ropes.'

The skipper looked hard at the boy.

'Well, the first one, anyway.' Robin looked slightly defiant.

'You saw him do it ?' Drew's eyes were ice-cold. 'Think hard. Much may depend on your answer.'

'No, I didn't see him do it. His back was towards me, but he could easily have——'

'That's enough, Trenchard. The rest is pure conjecture. Suspicion is one thing, proof another. Come, we are wasting time. It matters little who caused this mess, McCann or the grounding. You and I suspect him, therefore we shan't trust him or give him an inch.'

'But, sir——'

'Well ?'

'Why can't we lock him up till the end of the trip ? If he is involved in a plot he will be powerless to act ; if it is a mistake, then we have acted in good faith and can apologise when it is all over.'

The skipper's face broke into a smile as he listened to the simple suggestion. 'And not know when or where the next blow may come from?' he asked, putting his head on one side. 'No, lad, McCann is cunning but unintelligent. He has all the deceit, all the craft of the common criminal, but he lacks the brain of the master mind. We are safe so far. McCann cannot get in touch with the shore till we reach Aberdovey, so that if someone is doing the planning for him it will be too late. On the other hand if he is running the show himself then, as I said, he is unintelligent and we are his match any day. Come, sit here, I have a plan which I believe will succeed.'

In the galley several of the boys were standing around the warm stove, talking in low, earnest voices.

'Look, Ballard, you can say what you darned well like, but there is something queer afoot on this ship. We know all the yarns about the perils of the sea, the dangers of ships and those who sail in them, but this is something different, a strangeness about the whole business which I, for one, don't like, and I reckon there are a few more who feel as I do. Am I right?'

Percy spun round to face the others. There was some shuffling of feet and a good deal of unintelligible mumbling. Finally Jackie Main piped up:

'Chester is right you know, Timothy. There are odd goings on in this ship. The feeling has been growing slowly all throughout the trip. It wouldn't be so bad if there was something we could pinpoint and say, "Here it is; this is wrong, explain it!" But we can't. Every single incident can be accounted for by bad luck or an error of judgement. Taken together, they make a pattern which is frightening because however you look at it the logical end seems the same—the destruction of *Venturer*, and of someone in her.'

When he finished speaking there was an uneasy silence, broken only by the creak of the ropes, the thrum of the wind aloft and the incessant lap of the water on the planks.

Timothy poked up the galley fire into a blaze, showing the worried faces of the crew, sending their distorted shadows flickering wildly round the white-painted bulkheads. For some seconds he did not reply. He wanted to make certain that he said the right thing, knowing that it was up to him to rally the boys once again behind Robin. When at last he spoke, his voice was pitched so low that each pair of ears had to strain to catch what he said.

'I know that what has been happening has no obvious explanation,' he said, 'and I agree that if the past record is anything to go on, then we must expect something pretty unpleasant to happen before we reach Aberdovey. I don't know why we are the object of these attacks or whatever you like to call them. But I do know this: I trust Captain Drew and Robin Trenchard. If they could have told us what was going on, they would have done so long ago. They must be worried not only by these strange happenings but by the fact that they have to face them alone.'

This aspect had obviously not occurred to the others. By their faces Timothy saw this and continued, pressing home his advantage:

'Tell you what. Let's have a vote on it. All

who trust Robin and the skipper—up hands !' He looked round. 'Carried unanimously. Now all we have to do is decide how best to help them.'

It had worked. The boys were once again lined up and ready to do anything demanded of them. They were not disloyal or devoid of spirit. All they wanted was to understand what was happening—and how Timothy agreed with them !

Down among his engines McCann was in a black fury. Yet again his schemes had gone wrong and once more it was due to the quick wits and superb seamanship of the boys. It wasn't the men who worried him. But the boys—they were becoming an obsession with him ; and he still had not located the plans.

When the vessel grounded on leaving Caernarvon he had forced the skipper's door. Once inside the cabin he had ransacked it, even cut open the settee covers, making it look as if the rent had been caused by the heavy paper-weight, but it had deceived no-one.

Now time was growing short and they would soon be at the bar. Once over the shallows into the deeper water of the estuary, they would be there in no time, with people swarming on board again. No, he thought ; he must get those papers by force. The time must be just right though, so that he could get away before the alarm was raised. He had been told to avoid direct violence at all costs ; but things had gone too far, and now—he patted the small automatic in his hip pocket. As he sat lost in his own thoughts he became aware of subdued voices somewhere aft by the Captain's cabin.

'Carefully now. Lock it up. Give me the key. This brief-case must not be out of my sight till we are safe ashore.' That was Drew's voice.

'So that's it,' the engineer muttered triumphantly. Wherever they had been hidden, the vital documents were now in a brief-case somewhere along aft. In a flash his mind was made up. The final move became crystal clear.

He would wait till the schooner was over the bar before making his bid. Then the channel would be narrow and the skipper unable to leave the ship. He would seize the case from Drew and shoot his way out if need be ; leap into the motor boat, operating the quick release gear as he did so, and by the time people had recovered their senses he would be rapidly falling astern to be swallowed up in the gloom which even now was setting in.

After that, it would be easy to beach the boat and join up with his accomplices at the old quarry—a spot decided upon—should all else fail. From there, the black Alvis would soon put miles between himself and Aberdovey. It was so simple, so elegant, thought McCann, quite worthy of his flair for management.

'Stand by to cross the bar!' The order rang out loud and clear.

'Both engines half ahead.'

'Half ahead two,' McCann reported almost joyously, so pleased was he with his own schemes. On deck, darkness was falling fast.

'Shan't make it in daylight, sir,' Mr Howarth observed.

'No,' the skipper replied, 'but it won't matter.

We'll cross the bar by dark and will have entered the straight channel up to the pier.'

'There's the pilot boat ahead now, sir.' Mr Rees joined the group aft.

'Ah, yes. Take all sail off her then. Make up and stow, fast as you can.'

'Aye, aye, sir. Down sail, for the last time. Look smart, me hearties!' Howarth bellowed.

The boys went to with a will, gathering in the billowing canvas as the ropes raced aloft, over the blocks and down again. The deck was a scene of wild activity as each person busied himself with his particular job. Under the fold of the mainsail Chester and Naylor met as if by accident.

'See Trenchard haul in the dinghy painter just now?' Squeak hissed.

'No. What of it?'

'Why would he do it just now?'

'Probably to keep it from fouling the screws as we slow up for the pilot,' Chester replied.

'Maybe it's just me—but it seemed so deliberate.'

'Never mind. Remember what we agreed and keep your eyes peeled.'

The two parted, each going about his own job again. Yes, thought Chester, as he hauled the main sheet up two blocks, I wonder just what it all means.

An hour later the pilot was aboard and *Venturer*, safely over the bar, was making her way slowly up the narrow path between the ever-shifting sand-banks of the Dovey Estuary. McCann climbed up from the engine-room and sauntered across to the rail.

'Just having a breath of fresh air, sir; the

paraffin fumes are pretty bad below,' he called to the Captain.

'Very well,' Drew replied.

Casual though his action appeared, McCann had taken in two things. One was that darkness had almost fallen ; the other, that in Drew's hand was a small, black brief-case, secured by a silver chain to his wrist. Though his eyes glowed and his heart beat faster, the engineer continued to appear relaxed. He glanced idly ahead, leaning out over the rail. Suddenly his body stiffened and he yelled.:

'A mine ! Quick. A mine, dead ahead ; you can see its horns—there ! ' He pointed to the dark patch a couple of hundred yards ahead.

As he had hoped, everyone rushed for'ard ; even the pilot, leaving Drew and the helmsman by the wheel. Quick as a flash McCann sprang towards Drew and snatched the case from his grasp. As the skipper made to resist, a knee in his stomach doubled him up. He never felt the revolver butt strike the base of his skull, and as he sank to the deck the engineer wrenched the chain which snapped at the wrist, tearing the skin badly when it did so.

Next instant he was amidships, pushing Squeak Naylor aside as he vaulted into the motor boat hanging outboard in its davits. Howarth dashed up and, leaning over, nippered the ropes of the fall, so preventing them from running.

'Wot you doin', mate ? ' he demanded. 'You can't go—ouch ! ' His voice rose to a scream while the blood spouted from his gashed hands.

Knowing that both falls must run clear and simultaneously, McCann had ensured this by almost severing the bos'n's fingers with a vicious blow of the fireman's axe which was a standard part of lifeboat equipment. A second whang knocked out the pin holding the release gear. With a tremendous splash, the hull struck the water and was instantly swept astern.

It was all over in less time than it takes to tell. The impact knocked McCann into the bottom of the boat. By the time he righted himself, the schooner was a vague shape in the gloom ahead. It was no trouble to start the engine. One swing and she was away. The tiller hard over, the small grey boat headed for the shore.

The case was too big and obvious to carry, so McCann forced the feeble locks with a screwdriver. Inside was a bundle of papers carefully wrapped in oilskin. He drew them out and with the aid of a small pencil torch gazed at his prize.

There was a piece of paper with writing upon it. Eagerly the engineer, now trembling with excitement, read : *Foiled again, McCann.* The letters danced before his eyes. In a rage quite terrible to behold he ripped open each succeeding layer of the package, but all were the same—plain paper, with no plans.

Mr McCann was still trembling, but it was not excitement which now agitated his body, but temper, together with disappointment and wounded pride to think that he, the great schemer, had fallen for a trick like that ! He quickly mastered his feelings. He couldn't return to the ship and anyway, something told him the plans were not there. But if not—then where ?

He eased back the throttle, put the boat about

and sat thinking. Suddenly he had it. The painter —the painter hanging over the counter. When he had been swept under the ship's stern he had seen it dangling there, with no dinghy on the end. Someone had left the ship silently before him, but that someone was in a sailing boat with no engine and they couldn't be very far away. He hadn't been meant to leave. The case was supposed to lure him on to stay aboard till it was too late.

His spirits were rising once more. All was not yet lost. He would get even with these boys at last. Oh yes, they should pay in double measure. He spun the craft round to head down river. With the engine running dead slow he drifted along waiting for the moon to come out, certain that its silvery brightness would reveal the white sail for which he was searching. After that, it would only be a matter of time.

For a while nothing happened, then the moon peeped through a narrow rent in the heavy covering to be gone again almost as soon as it had emerged. But it was enough. McCann had seen it—a white blur on the port bow. With a low snarl he reached forward to jab the throttle wide open. The boat leapt forward.

Away out ahead, Robin should have been alone in the dinghy, but as it turned out there were three of them. He had been in the act of slipping away when Chester and Ballard had appeared from nowhere. Split seconds counted, so with no time to argue, Robin had been forced to take them with him.

To begin with, all had gone well, till they heard the unmistakable chug-chug of the motor-boat engine. They sat frozen like statues, but it had turned away towards the land. Robin continued telling the others the bare facts, so far as was necessary, when Percy suddenly said :

'Listen ! The boat engine has been eased back.'

They all strained to hear the motor. 'It has gone about, and seems to be coming this way.' Ballard cupped his ear to windward as he spoke. There was silence for some time, then the moon broke through for an instant. The engine roared, closer now ; and the chase was on.

As darkness descended Robin gave the order : 'Ready about'. He spun the little vessel round, steadying her on a course which would take them far out over the flats of the estuary.

'What's happened ?' Timothy whispered.

'Don't know,' Robin replied. 'Something must have gone wrong and McCann is after us now. We can't make shore on the other tack, so we will have to work to windward.'

In the power boat, the engineer forged ahead under full throttle. After five minutes he slowed down again, however, when the dinghy failed to show up. Cursing the cloud which covered the moon, he peered in vain into the darkness. A fresh breeze whipped up a steep sea, but it also kept the gaps in the sky moving. Away to the south-west a light patch of water seemed to draw nearer with unbelievable slowness. It was on his beam and of little interest to McCann since the dinghy was somewhere ahead. Glancing idly at the silver spot, he was astounded to see the white sails floodlit as the moon passed overhead.

'Confound them !' he bellowed. 'They have

altered course.' As he raved, he opened the engine up again, heading the boat towards where the sails had been. The boys heard the roar and all three turned to look as the boat came round.

'He's seen us again,' said Robin. 'Put her about.'

Timothy did so. Silently, the little craft slipped away from where the moon had found her. With bated breath her crew listened as their pursuer crossed astern of them to go racing off at right angles to their own course.

'Whew! That was a near one,' gasped Percy. 'I wonder how long we can keep this up.'

'Got it!' Robin slapped the thwart. 'Chester, you have been lapping up the chart. How soon after high water do these flats dry out again?'

Back in the other boat McCann was again lost. No sooner did he spot them than the moon would go and they would alter course. He tried various ways of catching them, of anticipating which way they would turn, but it didn't work. He was no seaman; the boys were. They were going farther and farther out into the bay, away from Aberdovey too, and this worried him.

Venturer would have anchored by now and the hunt would be on for him. He gazed anxiously at the fleeting clouds. If only the moon would come through for a reasonable time, he could end this nonsense.

'Reckon we are far enough to windward now, Robin, and the right distance out from the channel,' Chester said.

'I hope so.' Robin's answer was grim. 'We are about to be floodlit for a long time. Look at that gap. Let her come round. Slack away both sheets. Now, head for that very dim light—it's Penhelig harbour—and keep your fingers crossed.'

McCann had seen the gap approaching. Always unstable, the tension of the past hours had told on him. He sat poised in the stern sheets, his foot on the throttle lever waiting for his quarry to show up. Had any of his former shipmates seen him at that moment they would have said he was mad.

When the first streaks of light struck the sails, McCann rounded on it to send his boat racing in pursuit. The boys heard him and a cold shiver ran through all on board. Both craft were visible now, so that it was possible to see the power boat's foaming stem as she came up hand over fist.

'Chester, I hope your calculations are right. You reckon these banks should dry about now?' Robin's voice sounded strained.

'That's right.' Percy's reply was almost inaudible. 'And we have only a few hundred yards to go to the edge of the deep water channel.'

McCann was coming up fast. They could see him crouched over the controls. Soon only feet separated the boats. He shouted and screamed at them to stop, but they managed to stay just out of reach. Robin was conscious of the wind slackening. 'Oh, please, please, not now,' he prayed.

The other boat had sheared out to starboard and was making a run straight at them. McCann had lashed the tiller. Brandishing an axe in his hand he stood in the bow ready to jump. The gap narrowed.

Suddenly there was a jolt. The three boys pitched forward on to the floor boards. The power boat shot past, missing them it seemed by the fraction of an inch. Robin was first on his feet. ' Quick ! ' he yelled. ' Haul up the centre board.'

With swift movements they snatched up the long board which projected beneath the keel. The sails filled as the wind drove the boat on again. Twenty yards to port they saw McCann feverishly trying to get his heavier boat afloat. His frantic efforts were useless. He was well and truly grounded on the fast falling tide !

Robin, Timothy and Percy almost wept for joy when they realised that their nightmare race with the madman was ended. As they sailed past he hurled the axe at them. It struck the gunwale and remained there for some moments quivering, a stark reminder of what might have happened to them had they fallen into his hands.

The rest was soon over. In the Penhelig hotel Captain Drew and a certain Major were waiting, the former still badly shaken from the blow which McCann had given him. The plans, which had never left Robin's body since he received them, were given to the major who at once left the hotel.

Drew was a man of few words. He shook each boy by the hand : ' Well done,' he said, ' all of you. Your country has reason to be proud of *Venturer*'s crew. Now nip along and get a bath. Your Headmaster will be here soon, and I shouldn't wonder if I have some explaining to do.'

When they had cleaned themselves up, the boys returned to the upstairs room overlooking the estuary. Captain Drew greeted them.

' I should like you to meet someone,' said he,

'someone who is very lucky to be alive. Mr McCann —these are the boys!'

Percy swallowed hard, then blurted out: 'McCann—then who is out there?' He pointed to the window.

'An impostor,' Drew replied. 'They kidnapped the real gentleman as soon as he arrived in Oban.'

A plane roared low overhead. As the sound died, a green Very light floated down from the darkness. 'That's that bit of it all right,' the skipper said. 'Now for our friend—look.'

A ring of lights was closing in steadily from the far shore towards the deep water where a seven-knot tide race flowed. 'That's the Home Guard and the Commandos,' Drew explained. 'They caught the other members of the gang in a black Alvis at a road block.'

'Why didn't he use a gun?' Timothy asked.

Drew smiled, put his hand in his pocket and laid a revolver on the table. 'He hadn't got one—not then, anyway. Squeak gently relieved him of it as he climbed over the side. It was sticking out of his hip pocket. Lucky for you fellows, I should say.'

Through the window, Robin saw the ring of lights drawing tighter and tighter. It made him shudder.

Printed in Great Britain by
Thomas Nelson and Sons Ltd, Edinburgh